Reap

What

You

Sow

By

Craig McCabe

Self-Published Titles

By

Craig McCabe

This is dedicated to my Mother and Father,
The Timex strikers, and all their families.

A special thanks goes to John Leslie.

This is a work of fiction but the times, dates, places, companies, and events surrounding the Timex strike are true.

If you live in the wolf's den long enough, you learn how to howl

– Alejandro Gillick

Chapter 1

When Tommy stepped down from the top bunk of his shared cell he had an aura around him. After twenty-two years inside there would be no more setbacks, no more appeal rejections, today was his official release date, and nothing or no one was going to come between him and his freedom.

He had entered the prison system when he was only eighteen years old, a fresh-faced, confused, and angry young man. Confused about his persecution for something he did not do and angry at a system that was supposed to protect him. The prison regime had nearly broken him but he evolved into a headstrong and confident young man.

Now, as he stood by the tiny sink, looking at his reflection in the metal mirror on the wall, there was calmness about him. He was always clean-shaven and had no tattoos or any distinguishing features. His hair had been greying in recent years but wearing it slick back from his face, it was mostly hidden. He had procured some scars over the years from various accounts of violence but even they were now blending into his pale skin. His eyes widened as he tilted his head back and flexed his trapezius muscles, showing his tough chilling expression, a look he had learned to perfect to become a natural part of his appearance.

"What about the rest of your gear?" Asked Speedy, his new cellmate

Tommy looked along the row of music tapes. There was a mixture of rock from the late seventies through to the early eighties. On tough days he liked to play them to help him reminisce of the old days, the innocent times of his childhood with no tainted memories of life in prison. The other prisoners would tease Tommy about his 'white boy music' but Tommy didn't mind.

"You keep it. You might need it." He winked

Speedy's real name was Curtis. He had gained his nickname after accepting the role of a getaway driver in several armed robberies. They had shared a cell for over six months, but to Tommy, he was still new, as his last cellmate was with him for nearly five years.

There was a row of various legal and political books and Tommy had read them all, some, several times over. There were posters, music tapes, and a large box containing court documents and files from his appeals. There were also letters from family and friends that he had cherished over the years and some from strangers that had read about his case and felt as though they should write to him to show their support. They were far from glory collectibles and he had no need for any of them now. In his hand were the only things that were important to him, his precious collection of photographs of his son. The previous night, he had bound them together with several elastic bands and held them tight in his hand.

Tommy heard the screw's footsteps and stood up close to the door. The keys jingled outside but they never entered the lock. The viewing hatch on the door slid open and when the screw's eyes peered through the gap, Tommy's aura quickly disappeared and he felt his stomach tighten. He could not handle another setback, not now, not this time. In the split second that it had taken the screw to start talking, Tommy had envisioned an all-out riot if he was refused his release.

In all his years inside, Tommy was not part of the prison hierarchy but he had their complete respect and at his nod, they would have happily taken control of the whole prison.

"Five minutes Tommy. We're dealing with a slight incident."

Tommy took a deep breath, he looked down and realised he was clutching his bundle of photographs so tightly that his thumb was making a dent. He stood back from the door, stretched up his neck and shoulders, and began pacing back and forwards in the cell, this was going to be the longest five minutes of his whole twenty-two years. He heard the screws keys jingle once more and he paused for a few seconds as he listened intently near the cell door but it stayed locked. He lifted his chest and inhaled a deep breath before turning on his heels to pace away from the door once again. As he turned, he locked eyes with Speedy as he lay on the bottom bunk watching him. He smiled up at Tommy nervously, not knowing if he was on the verge of exploding, Tommy did not smile back. He paced some more and when he turned to face him a second time it was Tommy who smiled, he kept pacing and breathing hard and trying his best to keep his hard expression. Tommy eventually could not hold it in any longer and his face burst into a wide smile that he could not shake off. It was infectious and Speedy was smiling with him. It had reached a point where each time Tommy turned on his heels to face him; they were both sniggering like little schoolboys.

The key turned in the lock and Tommy stopped pacing, he stood in the middle of the cell, still breathing hard, and watched the door. His smile dropped when he turned to face Speedy for the last time.

"I've waited on this day for so long, I'm now fucking scared to leave."

Speedy stood up from his bunk and they both hugged.

"All the best Tommy, take care."

"You too, remember what I told you, study, study anything and everything. Keep your mind occupied, and keep it sharp."

"Will do" He nodded and lay back on his bunk still smiling.

Tommy walked out of his cell, his calm aura had returned. Due to whatever incident the screws were dealing with, the whole block had been in lockdown. Although he would have liked to have seen some of the inmates one last time, it was no big deal. He had said his goodbyes the previous day. As he walked slowly along the gantry, he heard the faint call of his name, by the time he reached the last security door to the hall; every prisoner was banging on their cell doors and chanting.

"Tommy, Tommy, Tommy"

Tommy's smile was wide and he had to hold back a tear or two as he exited the prison. Once outside, he stood for a few seconds and took a few deep breaths. At this moment, he was unsure of his long-term future, but one thing he was certain about, was that whatever it involved, he did not intend on coming back here. His biggest fear was being institutionalised. He had known prisoners who committed violent crimes within weeks or even days of their release just so that they could go back inside. Tommy let all these thoughts pass, as at this precise moment, he had something more important to attend to, making up for the lost time between him and his son.

Over the years, there had been many requests on Tommy's behalf for a transfer to a prison closer to his hometown in Dundee. His solicitor had pleaded for sympathy as Tommy felt isolated due to being so far away and the distance made it difficult for family or friends to visit him. The authorities, without any explanation, rejected his request. His mother and father still made the journey twice, sometimes three times a year and he had the occasional visit from old friends who had kept in touch, and as much as Tommy appreciated their sentiments, he knew they all had their own lives to live. In recent years though, the only visit he looked forward to, was from his son, Liam.

Liam was only a baby when Tommy was first sent to prison and although he never expected Jade, his ex-girlfriend to bring him the hundreds of miles to visit him, he was hurt and angry when she denied a request by his parents to take him, even more so when she stated that if they took him without her permission, she would stop contact altogether. Tommy put on a brave face for the sake of his parents but inside he was furious. The photographs he received were his only salvation. He had enough to deal with inside without having the added pressure of losing contact with his son. After a few years, Tommy was able to talk to Liam on the phone which became more frequent as he grew older and once Liam learned to write, he would send Tommy letters describing his day-to-day activities. Tommy longed for the letters but more so the photographs. He would stare at his most recent photograph for hours and let his mind drift off to help him escape from his predicament. He would imagine a different life where he would be by his son's side, teaching him how to ride a bike or helping him with his homework.

In one of Tommy's phone calls to Liam, when he had come to an age where he had begun to ask questions, he randomly asked Tommy why he did not want him to come and visit him. Tommy changed the subject and said goodbye. He cut short his long-awaited phone call and hung up the receiver as he did not want Liam to hear the hurt in his voice. He was stunned that Jade would tell his son something so hurtful. He walked back to his cell to compose himself, returning moments later to call Jade. He used all his control to put his anger aside and told her calmly that if she did not stop telling his son lies about him, he would start telling him the truth about her. The conversation with Liam did not come up again. By the time Liam had turned sixteen, he was desperate to visit his father, and there was nothing legally his mother could do.

That first visit was extremely difficult for Tommy. It was the first time he had embraced his son since he was a baby and he wanted to cry. He saw it in his son's eyes, he also wanted to cry, but as they both glanced around the hall at the other prisoners and the observing screws, a quick hug was about as emotional as they could get considering their surroundings. They sat down opposite each other and for the next hour, they talked. It was small talk, nothing deep, they laughed and joked and they both realised that they had the same sense of humour, the same sarcastic humour that Jade detested. Liam was sixteen and was already much taller than Tommy, he was practically a grown man. That first visit had not only made him think about how much he had missed out on his own life but also the best years of his son's life.

Tommy did not receive many visits and as he looked around the hall, he caught sight of some of the prisoners watching him. In the months leading up to his first visit with Liam, Tommy's anxiety had been building up, the other prisoners noticed it and so did the screws. His anxiety was not only about seeing Liam, but also about Liam seeing him. Tommy had been like a ticking time bomb and he was slowly starting to crack. He had fought every day for his freedom since being locked up, whether it was studying so that he could understand the court proceedings or fighting to survive in a sometimes hostile environment, but in the months leading up to that first visit, Tommy felt as though he was on the verge of giving up. Like any long-term prisoner, there are only so many disappointments that a person can take before they start to lose their mind. When a prisoner like Tommy is denied parole for no apparent reason, it can sometimes be enough to send them over the edge. The build-up to each appeal and the instant decisions against Tommy had taken a lot out of him. It was hard, and some days he fought within to stop himself from going crazy, but after that first visit with his son, something came over him. A calmness, an inner control that he carried throughout the rest of his sentence.

Over the years, new lawyers would take up Tommy's case and they could never understand why the judges would reject his appeals without even a hint of consideration. Tommy knew though, and when none of the appeal judges would listen to his plea, he would accept their decision and move on to fight it another day. He studied hard on the ins and outs of Law. He pursued every avenue of his case and even though it was all to no avail, he would never give them the satisfaction of giving up and rotting away, Tommy fought the decision to the very last day of his sentence.

Chapter 2

On the advice of the screws, Tommy stood by the nearest bus stop. He took in long deep breaths of the clean fresh air and let it fill his lungs. Although he had an allocated time in the prison yard for exercise every day, this was different. The air outside the prison walls was not tainted with the fears, anxieties, or angry thoughts of the other prisoners.

Upon Tommy's release, Liam had originally planned to travel down to meet him but Tommy had requested him not to do this. Liam knew he had his reasons but was still sceptical so pressed his father further for an explanation. To Tommy, this did not seem like a conversation he should be having with his son, and was a little hesitant in divulging the truth.

"Liam, I haven't been with a woman in twenty-two years."

Liam smiled but was worried, worried that his father's first port of call was a venture that would likely lead him straight back to prison.

Tommy boarded the bus and sat close to the window. He stared out at the world with wide eyes at how much it had changed. The only time Tommy had ever stepped beyond the prison walls was for one of his many court appeals. He was transported in a large security van and was occasionally accompanied by other prisoners who were also attending court that day. If Tommy stretched up in the van while it was moving, he would sometimes catch a glimpse of the outside world through one of the small square windows but his mind was usually far too occupied to take advantage of this.

Tommy stepped off the bus in the busy city and looked up the street, the sign he was looking for had not changed, if anything it had only gotten bigger and there was certainly no mistaking the large M of McDonald's. If there was one specific type of food that he craved while being inside it was a McDonald's burger. He had watched a show many years ago in prison, about a man on death row in America, his last meal was a burger from McDonald's and Tommy sympathised. As he walked up the street, he felt as though everyone was in a hurry for something as they all rushed past him in both directions. He pulled open the large glass doors and joined the queue. While making his way down the line he scanned the menu on the large screen ahead of him but there was no need, he knew exactly what he was going to order, it was the death row meal.

"Next, please. What can I get you?" The girl said in a broken English accent.

Tommy picked it up as Eastern European. He had come across many of them in prison, more so in recent years. If their accent was strong enough, he could sometimes work out their exact origin, although he was unsure of the girl serving, she had been communicating in English for some time now. When he recited his order, it made him think of his own accent, it had changed somewhat over the years but Tommy had not noticed. Having been in the company of some strong English accents, Tommy still sounded Scottish, but when he talked to his parents or any of his old friends, they would comment on his now English accent.

The girl slid the tray with his meal towards him and Tommy checked it over, two burgers, two large fries and two large milkshakes of different flavours. As he turned around, he quickly scanned the seating area and noticed a vacant seat close by, but Tommy had his seat picked out the minute he walked in the door. It was by the far wall, specifically chosen so that he was less exposed and could see who was coming and going. He sat down and looked over his food. He did not know where to start. He took a sip from both of the milkshakes. The sweet taste was exactly as he had remembered. He leaned forward to take a bite of his burger and his eyes moved from side to side, watching his surroundings intently. He did this with every bite. Whenever someone close by made a sudden movement, his eyes would dart in their direction. His institutional habits were going to be difficult to change. Tommy kept thinking of the person on death row, and just like him, he was savouring every bite. He cleared his tray and stepped outside, once again, taking long deep breaths of fresh air.

Speedy had given him specific directions and arranged everything for him several weeks before his release. Tommy remembered the names of the side streets but had now come to a point where he felt a little disorientated and that he had maybe taken a wrong turn. Speedy explained that it would not be a problem to stop and ask for directions as according to him, the place was like a landmark. Tommy had a sharp memory so began to get more confused by the second as to where he had gone wrong, he turned on his heels and looked back up the street. After slowly working his way back down, he noticed the sign a short distance from where he stood. The Groundhog, as he relaxed in a slow stride up the street, he thought about the pub name and wondered if the owner had taken it from the movie of a similar name, Groundhog Day, which was ironically, the last movie he had seen at the cinema before his time in prison. The doors of the pub were jammed open and there were three people gathered outside having a smoke, something Tommy had still to get used to. He stepped inside and due to the time being close to lunch, most of the tables were either busy or had a small reserve plaque placed on them. Tommy went straight to the bar and ordered a pint. The barmaid served him and upon her return with his change, Tommy asked her in a soft polite manner. "I was wondering if Trevor was in today."

"Yeah sure, I'll just go and give him a shout. Who will I say is asking?"

"Tommy, Tommy Ross."

"He's very busy as you can imagine but I'll let him know you are here?"

"That would be great, thanks."

Tommy noticed a stool further along the bar, at first he considered moving but if he sat there it would have meant his back was to the customers and manoeuvring the stool closer to where his pint was, would attract too much attention, so he decided to stay put. He started with small sips of his pint, slowly appreciating the taste, this evolved to large gulps and he was soon ordering another. After the barmaid served up his second pint, a tall burly man appeared from behind the bar with a welcoming smile.

“Tommy Ross?”

Tommy nodded.

“I’m Trevor.” The man put his hand out for Tommy to shake. Tommy returned it with a smile.

“Come on back. You can bring your pint with you.”

Tommy walked through the open hatch of the bar and followed Trevor through to the back of the pub. He opened a door to a set of stairs which led to an adjoining flat, Trevor’s flat.

“Have a seat I’ll be back in a minute.”

Tommy sat in the middle of the sofa and looked around the room. It was basic but clean, with some pub memorabilia on the walls. Trevor appeared with a small notebook and sat down opposite Tommy.

“So what are you into?” He said as he flicked through the pages.

“What do you mean?”

“Young, old, big tits, black?”

“I’m not sure.”

Trevor smiled. “Would you like me to pick someone for you?”

Tommy nodded. “I suppose it doesn’t matter what she’s like, I probably won’t last too long anyway.”

They both forced a smile.

Trevor used his index finger to guide him down the page of his book. I have someone here who will be perfect for you. She is early thirties and has a great body. Also, she doesn’t go for any of that weird shit and will be real gentle.”

Tommy shrugged “Sounds good.”

Trevor picked up the phone and dialled her number.

"Hey Sonia, its Trevor ...Yeah, hi, are you available? It's for a friend …at the pub …sure, yeah twenty minutes, ok just come around the back"

Trevor hung up. "She won't be long." He gave Tommy a satisfied nod before he reached into his pocket and pulled out a small wrap. He placed it on the coffee table next to Tommy's pint.

"It's on me" He winked.

Tommy had managed to avoid the trap of drugs in prison. He had dabbled here and there but it had mostly been out of curiosity than any sort of peer pressure. He was not keen on it as it gave him an agitated feeling and hindered his concentration when he was reading or studying. He understood why other prisoners liked it though.

Drugs changed everything in prison, Tommy didn't mind a bit of puff, he occasionally had a smoke with some of the older guys but it wasn't his thing. He liked to keep a clear mind and not let his guard down. He couldn't, not in that place. A prisoner only had to turn their back for a split second to end up in a bad way. When other drugs began to appear in prison, it made Tommy angry, on edge, even more so than he already was. The last ten years had been the worst for it due to the influx of synthetic drugs that were flooding the prisons. These new drugs could go undetected by the scanners and sniffer dogs and the more drugs that were smuggled in, the more dealers it produced, which in turn caused more violence. Tommy was glad to get out.

Tommy sipped his pint and placed it down next to the wrap. He then leaned back in the chair leaving the wrap in its place. Trevor could tell that Tommy was hesitant so leaned forward emptying the white powder from the warp onto the table. He used a credit card to divide the powder into four lines. He rolled up a note and offered it to Tommy. Tommy nodded back at him and Trevor stood up to lean over the table and snort one of the lines. He handed the note to Tommy. The note had come loose so Tommy re-rolled it tightly and snorted one of the lines. Back in 1993 before Tommy became imprisoned, cocaine was not as accessible as it was now. His only knowledge back then had been what he had seen on TV and when it had started to emerge in prison, it was cut so much that his expectations were left wanting and he did not understand what the fuss was about. Tommy relaxed back into the chair, and within minutes, he knew this was different. His face went slightly numb and he felt the same agitated state that he had experienced before, only this time it was much stronger.

"Listen, Tommy, I'll have to go and check on a few things downstairs, I won't be long. Do you want another pint?"

"Sure, thanks."

Trevor left and Tommy sat quietly sipping his pint.

Moments later, Tommy was on his feet looking around the room. A paranoid feeling came over him that this whole thing was a set-up to put him back in prison. He had placed his trust in Speedy that he would not put him in this position, but Trevor appeared to be a little too cavalier for Tommy's liking. He took a deep breath and put his conflicting thoughts aside as he sat down and took another drink from his pint. His heart was racing but he was beginning to enjoy the feeling. He savoured the rest of his pint and stood up to go looking for the toilet. Upon his return, a girl was sitting in his seat. She looked to be around her late twenties, peroxide blond and a little on the heavy side. She was done up to look very professional in a suit jacket with a blouse tied together with a large bow, If Tommy had not pre-known this arrangement he would have taken her to be a businesswoman of some kind. Tommy sat opposite in Trevor's vacated seat where a fresh pint was waiting for him.

"Hi, I'm Sonia, Trevor asked me to bring that up for you" She smiled.

"Thanks" He leaned over and tilted the glass to take a sip without removing it from the table.

When he glanced up he caught a glimpse of Sonia's legs, they were tanned and slim, much slimmer than her top half would suggest. His eyes followed them up to where they met with her short skirt. Tommy had not encountered many women since being locked up and out of those that he had, whether they were lawyers or secretaries, nurses or even some inmate's wives in the visiting room, he could not recollect any of them with a skirt so short.

Tommy wondered how this was going to start, was he the one to make a move? Was he to ask her what she does? Was she going to strip? The questions raced through his head until Sonia stood up, picked up a cushion from the sofa and walked around the table towards Tommy. She let the cushion fall to his feet before kneeling in front of him. She placed her hands on his thighs and Tommy tensed up.

"Are you okay?"

"Yeah, just a little nervous, it's been a while."

Sonia gave him a warm smile and gently rubbed her hands towards Tommy's groin. He felt a tingle of excitement come over him and by the time Sonia had opened the buttons on his jeans, he was already hard. She gestured for him to slide forward and seconds later his penis was in her mouth. Tommy watched her head move slightly up and down and he knew he wasn't going to last long. He tapped her on the shoulder to stop.

"Is everything okay?"

"Yeah it's great, it's just...can you stand up a second?"

As Sonia rose to her feet, Tommy turned her around and shuffled towards the sofa with his jeans still at his ankles. He bent her over and pulled her skirt up over her waist revealing her lace knickers. He slid them down gently and entered her from behind. With both hands, Tommy grabbed a tight hold of her skirt and began thrusting. Minutes later he made a low grunting sound and pulled away. After pulling up his jeans he sat back down on the chair. Sonia fixed herself and smiled at Tommy before vacating the room. Tommy reached for his pint and took a long slow sip. He was now felt ready for the long journey to go and meet his son.

Chapter 3

Tommy boarded the Edinburgh-bound train at King's Cross. The carriages were fairly empty and he chose a seat by the window facing the direction the train was travelling. Several stops later, whilst still in the London district, the train was almost full and he was now sharing his window seat with a young couple. With so many people on board, Tommy's anxiety was beginning to surface. As the train travelled north towards Newcastle a young lady wearing tight sports clothes was sitting at a table across the aisle from Tommy. She had purchased a sandwich and a bottle of water from the catering trolley and looked like she was having trouble opening the plastic carton that contained the sandwich. Tommy stared over. He was close to asking if she needed help until the plastic lid flipped up. Tommy was more relieved than the young lady. She took a small bite and placed it back in the carton and closed the lid. She then opened the plastic bottle and took a sip. Tommy watched as she toyed with the lid of the bottle, and only after securing it back on the bottle did she decide to open it again and take another sip. Each time she did this Tommy's anxiety would flare up. He tried to block it out until she picked up the sandwich carton once again. The noise of the plastic being pressed constantly was driving Tommy mad.

His anxiety was brought on by another disorder called Misophonia, a condition where certain sounds can trigger an emotional or physiological response. Tommy had researched the condition while inside, even discussing some of the symptoms with the prison Doctor, but not so far as to explain that certain noises made him feel violent. Over the years, he had encountered most noises that triggered his Misophonia and found ways of dealing with them, but the crunching plastic was something new.

Tommy wanted to shout at her to hurry up and eat her fucking sandwich but decided it was probably best to move seats rather than make a scene. He stood up and walked to the next carriage. Most of the seats with tables were busy but he found a vacant seat at the far end. When the train arrived in Newcastle more passengers were exiting than entering and this made the rest of his journey to Edinburgh more pleasant.

Tommy had an hour to wait for his connecting train to Dundee and after an over-priced cup of coffee and a short stretch of the legs along princess street for a view of the castle, Tommy was soon back in the station. It was now rush hour and the platform was extremely busy. When Tommy entered the nearest carriage it was already full. He spotted an empty aisle seat with a rucksack and wondered if it was taken. Next to it was a casually dressed man opposite a female and young child. Due to their interaction, Tommy surmised that they were together. He about turned to go through to the next carriage when through the glass doors, he spotted several people standing. Tommy decided to stay put.

"Excuse me, sir, is anyone sitting there?" Tommy nodded to the seat with the rucksack.

"No go ahead" The man removed the rucksack and placed it under the table by his feet.

As the minutes ticked by and the passengers waited patiently to depart, more and more people entered the train. Tommy glanced around to see a small group gathered in the aisle by the luggage rack behind him, and his anxiety arose again. Tommy rested his head back and tried to relax, he was relieved that he decided to take the seat.

When the train arrived in Dundee, Tommy took his time and let the crowd rush out in front of him. As he followed behind them through the station towards the exit, he felt an aura surround him once again, only this time the feeling was stronger, much stronger. The only way he could describe it would be to compare it with a kid on Christmas morning, rushing downstairs to a pile of presents. He reached the stairway that led up to the exit barrier and when he looked up he saw Liam, towering over the crowd. Tommy walked up the steps and saw the emotion on Liam's face, it told him everything. When Tommy stepped through the barrier he reached out and pulled Liam towards him. They had embraced many times over the years but this was different. They had waited twenty-two years for this moment and every emotion that Liam held back in those prison visits had now risen to the surface. No screws were breathing down their necks, nobody listening in to their conversations, and no snide glances from other inmates, but mostly, there were no time restraints.

Liam was parked a short distance from the train station "Did you ever learn how to drive Dad?"

"You know that is something that never really crossed my mind. I'll need to put it on my list of things to do."

"That must be a long fucking list" Liam smiled.

With Tommy's condition flaring up on the train he thought that maybe avoiding public transport would help his anxiety. He took a mental note to place 'learning to drive' near the top of his list.

Liam pointed towards his works van.

"Liam's mobile car valet" Tommy was impressed.

The van was nothing special, but seeing his son's name on his own business, he couldn't have felt more proud. Liam drove through the city centre and along the waterfront to show Tommy how much the city had changed. Tommy tried his hardest to remember some of the buildings but it had been too long and the city had changed so much since he left.

"I want to go past my old flat up Ardler."

"Ardler was demolished in the late nineties, Dad."

"Yeah, I know. I still want to see it."

"Gran and Grandad are expecting you."

"It's okay, they'll understand."

Liam exited the ring road and made his way east out of the city centre. It was not until they approached the Lochee area that the streets were becoming familiar to him, he recognised some of the buildings and Liam drove slowly to let Tommy take it all in. When they reached the fly-over towards Camperdown Park, Liam caught Tommy filling his cheeks with air before slowly breathing out.

“Are you okay?”

“Yeah, I’m mentally preparing myself for what’s around this corner” Tommy joked.

Liam didn’t need to ask what he meant. He didn’t know the exact details or the extent of his father’s involvement, only what he had managed to dig up in old newspapers after hearing snippets of conversations while growing up. He turned off Coupar Angus Road and made a turn onto Faraday Street. As Liam ascended the hill, Tommy’s eyes were firmly focused on the factory to his left. Even with the large Timex sign vacant from the building, it still gave Tommy a chill when he saw it. Liam took a left onto Harrison Road and Tommy had a slight shiver when he passed the factory gates, the crowds of angry women shouting and screaming at the scab buses were still vivid after all those years.

1991

It was the morning of Tommy’s interview and the job was for an unskilled assembly line worker. His mother, who also worked there, had arranged it, and although it appeared to be a formality, Tommy was still nervous. He had been unemployed for several months now and his only work experience was a short period on the government's Youth Training Scheme. A program where employers would sign up to take on school leavers aged sixteen to eighteen and the government would pay their wages for the first two years. This was intended to be an incentive for the employer to offer the applicant a full-time contract once the two years were completed. There were several major flaws in this new scheme and one was that the wages were no more than what the government was handing out in unemployment benefits, thus the applicant was doing a full week of work for a pittance and the employer used the applicant for two years of free labour before finding a feeble excuse to sack them before their trial period was up. Tommy had three Y.T.S. placements in the space of six months, with one of them lasting less than a week. Due to Tommy looking young for his age, he was prone to bullying and while certain members of staff attempted to take advantage of Tommy, they soon found that he did not take to intimidation lightly and Tommy was ordered back to the agency to be replaced with another reluctant applicant. After Tommy's third and final placement, he was now in the same situation as his friends who had no money, slept late and hung around the shops most nights causing some sort of disruption. Tommy's father was constantly on his case to get up and find a job, any job. Tommy felt under pressure, he was desperate and was even close to signing up for the army. His father was all for it and thought it would do him good, but when this was mentioned to his mother, she feared her son would be sent to the troubles in Northern Ireland and so pressed the management into giving him a job in the factory where she worked. After borrowing a shirt and tie for his interview, Tommy made his way to the Timex factory on Harrison Road.

The Timex was an American business, an international brand that came to Dundee in 1946. The workers were well paid and they enjoyed good bonuses. By the mid-sixties, Timex had three factories in Dundee, Milton of Craigie, Dunsinane Avenue and Harrison Road. In the early seventies, at its peak, it employed around 7000 people, a huge number for a small city. Towards the end of the seventies, this number was reduced to 5000 and by the early eighties the employee numbers were reduced further but they were still the largest employer in the city above NCR and Levis

The Timex was a large part of Dundee that employed generations of the same families and after a successful interview; Tommy was now part of this tradition. His job was only temporary but if he was still employed after two years, by law, the company would have to offer him a full-term contract. Tommy was optimistic about the job even though the two years scenario struck a chord with him. He knew all too well that large companies abused this system by terminating an employee days before their two-year contract was up, to then re-employ them the following day with another two-year temporary contract. Tommy loved the job, it was decent pay for easy work and there was always plenty of overtime. He was also making new friends of different age groups instead of hanging around the shops with his friends being a nuisance.

Chapter 4

The Ardler housing estate previously contained six multi-storey blocks that were demolished along with several maisonette blocks and walk-up type flats to make way for new semi-detached houses.

As Liam reached the far end of Harrison Road and crossed over Rosemount Road to enter the Ardler estate, he caught Tommy leaning forward in his seat as though stretching to look into the sky.

"No multis?"

"No, they're long gone. I'm sure I read somewhere that the first multi came down in ninety-three."

"The year you were born."

"Apparently It was a rough area around the time the factory closed, high unemployment, people were pissing in the lifts, vandalising the lights, drug use was on the up and pensioners were scared to leave their homes. They regenerated the whole area."

"What's it like now?"

"Pretty much the same" They both smiled.

Tommy stretched his neck out to the side and looked all around him. Liam continued driving through the estate, passing the shops and the community centre. Tommy was struck by the changes. He tried to place things in his mind as they were before and when Liam drove back onto Rosemount Road Tommy told him to pull over. They both got out of the car and Liam watched Tommy stare all around him.

"What is it? What are you thinking?"

Tommy positioned himself to face back up towards Harrison Road "Right there" Tommy pointed "That's where my flat was. That was where you were born, well, you were born in the hospital but this was your first address."

"I know, I looked it up"

"I remember that time like it was yesterday."

Liam looked at his father and caught a slight sadness in his eyes.

Tommy had another look around before getting back into the car.

1992

Tommy had known Jade from school, she was part of the crowd that hung around the local shops and Tommy liked her. They had started dating casually around the time Tommy took the job at Timex. Three months later, Jade broke the news to him that he was going to be a father. Tommy's outlook on life changed overnight. He put his name down for a place to live and began working overtime several nights a week and most weekends. He stopped hanging around the shops at night and he barely saw any of his friends. He was offered the keys to a flat in a walk-up style block which was only a short distance from the factory. When Tommy and Jade opened the door to their new home they smiled.

"Not bad, some wallpaper and a coat of paint and it will be perfect" Tommy understated.

Tommy began decorating straight away and even on nights when he was working overtime, he still went to the flat after work to continue. Some nights he was there until after midnight but would still make it to work on time the following day. He was exhausted and people around him were telling him to slow down, but Tommy was determined he would have everything in place for when the baby arrived.

When Tommy and Jade moved into the flat, everything seemed to be falling into place. They both seemed content in their surroundings and with Tommy living so close to the factory he would quickly nip home on his lunch break to see Jade. It was a happy and exciting time for both of them.

It was the week leading up to the Christmas break and Jade was going out for the day so Tommy decided to have his lunch in the factory. On the way to the canteen, he clocked the queue by the office where some of the workers were waiting in line to pick up their payslips early, instead of waiting for them to be handed around the factory later in the day. Tommy was in no hurry for his lunch and decided to join the queue. He had worked so much overtime the previous week that he was in the factory for more hours than he was out of it. He was excited to see his wage slip, and as he stood in the queue his mind was in deep thought of what he could buy Jade for Christmas, he had not noticed the sullen faces walking passed him. Having only recently become of age to be taxed, Tommy was hesitant upon opening his payslip but his face soon broke into a wide smile, there was no need for the worry as the amount far exceeded his expectations. The wage slip had come with a letter attached and Tommy assumed that it was details about his new tax code. He opened the letter and his smile immediately dropped from his face. It was a letter to inform him that as of the end of the working week, he would no longer be employed by the Timex Corporation. Along with all the temporary staff being terminated, there were also plans to lay off half of the full-time staff.

Tommy didn't take it too seriously, it was no big deal, he was sure his mother would fix it for him to return. Even if it took a few weeks, she would put in a word or pull a few strings to get him back in. They knew he was a hard worker and could put in the hours when asked. Tommy sat down to eat his lunch and saw the panic on the worker's faces as they discussed the lay-offs. He didn't let it bother him; he would still enjoy his Christmas and New Year with Jade. They wouldn't exactly be out partying much with her being pregnant. They would get by as he had earned enough to tide them over for a few weeks.

1993

After the Christmas break, when the full-time staff returned to work, the management offered them a new contract. It contained details that meant they would be working more hours for less pay and understandably, the workers refused to sign it. Most of the workers were part of a union, the Amalgamated Engineering and Electrical Union.

The A.E.E.U. is an association of workers formed to represent employees in all matters of law, and through elected leadership, their purpose is to negotiate with employers to improve pay, benefits, health and safety, complaint procedures, promotions, terminations and working conditions.

The negotiations between the union and the management about the working conditions, the cut in wages, the planned lay-offs, and also the cut in pensions continued throughout the week. During this time, the employees still turned up for work each day, optimistic that the union would smooth out a deal and get things back on track.

At the end of that first week, the Timex workers received a letter from the management with their payslips. The letters were either thick or thin, the thin letter meant that their job was safe and the thick letter contained details on how to claim benefits as they were being laid off. The usual policy of last in first out was not applied as the management had hand-picked the employees that would have made the greatest protest including the union activists to be included in the lay-offs. This was a clear attempt at breaking the union. They had proposed a rotational workforce but the bosses were adamant they wanted it reduced. The workers refused to accept the letters and occupied the canteen. The president of Timex, Mr Peter Hall, promised more negotiations and even though a ballot showed the workers were 92% in favour of a strike, the union accepted the principle of lay-offs and they returned to work.

Tommy's mother called him to explain that things were not looking good for him returning to work anytime soon and it would be wise if he started to look elsewhere for work. Tommy was distraught, he knew there was not much-unskilled work around and now that he was eighteen, he would be considered too old to start an apprenticeship.

Friday 8th – 29th January

The workers were on rotating shifts to cover their laid-off workmates as they waited for further negotiations that never came. While the unions were proposing the lay-offs to be on a rotational basis, the management was firm that they wanted the workforce reduced. With their pleas ignored, they sought advice from the Advisory Conciliation and Arbitration Service (ACAS). A government organisation was formed to help improve performance and solve working relations problems, but this was also ignored. Frustrated by the constant uncertainty and despite an intervention by officials of the A.E.E.U. the workers came out on strike.

Sunday 31st of January

The union organised a meeting at the Marryat Hall in the city centre for all workers, they informed them that they were on strike illegally and the ones that had received the thin letters were to start back the next working day. Also discussed at this meeting was the occupation of the Timex Plant in Milton back in 1983, where the workers carried out an occupation of the factory that involved a six-week sit-in which saved 1900 jobs. The workers decided that whatever proposals were put to them, they would all stick together.

Monday 1st February

They assumed the rotating shifts would carry on and there would be more talks but when the workers turned up at the factory that Monday morning, the gates were locked. Excluding office staff, the management refused entry to all 343 workers, thus making any planned sit-in impossible. A twenty-four-hour picket line was set up and the media were informed.

The negotiations continued and despite an offer to return to work while the negotiations were ongoing, the management tried to change the conditions further by insisting that any return to work was dependent on the workers taking a ten per cent pay cut, a massive reduction in their pension provision, an end to a range of benefits and also reduced union representation. The union put this offer to the workers, who did not accept the conditions.

Friday 5th February

The workers received letters which were hand delivered by a local taxi company, Toft Hill Cabs, to inform them that their employment was now terminated. There was a public outcry and massive support for the workers.

Monday 8th February

It was only days after the workers received their termination letters that the first replacement workers were being bussed in through the Timex gates. Due to these replacement workers not being employed by the company before the dispute, they were classed as strike-breakers, more widely known as Scabs, people who cross a picket line to work in defiance of strikers. The hire of Scabs had been preplanned by Hall for some time, and only once the interviews were completed, the hire of buses and the arrangement of pick-up points were in place, he sacked the workers.

Chapter 5

Tommy had always been an early riser, even when he had nothing in particular to get up for, he would still wake up at first light. For several days now, he had been intrigued by the angry roar of chants that had been interrupting his morning coffee and decided to investigate. He looked out of the window to see a white sheet of frost on the ground and wrapped up tightly. After checking in on Jade, who was still sleeping soundly, he made his way towards the factory. As he approached the gates he saw his mother in amongst the crowd of workers that appeared to be mostly women. He was about to cross over the road to see them when a car came speeding up the hill. Tommy stood on the edge of the kerb to let it pass when at the last second the driver put his indicator on and abruptly came to a halt at the gates. The workers, upon seeing this, immediately raised their arms and began shouting furiously 'SCAB' while the security rushed to open the gate to allow them through. Tommy stood in shock, his mother, in those few seconds, had changed from the small timid woman he had known his whole life to what he could only describe as an angry Pitbull. Once the car was through the gates, he crossed over and was welcomed into the crowd with wide smiles from his mother and her workmates.

"Tommy, how is the job hunting going?"

"Great, I have an interview for here later" He joked.

"I wouldn't joke about that. This lot will have you strung up next to those overalls on those trees"

They both glanced up at the line above them where several strikers' overalls fluttered in the wind above them. Another car appeared and the chants of 'SCAB' started once again. The car stopped at the gates and Tommy noticed the passengers covering their faces to hide their identities. The driver had no qualms whatsoever about what he was doing or where he was going as he sat almost smug-like watching the angry scene around him. Tommy caught him smirk as he drove past the security. With the freezing temperatures starting to bite, Tommy had seen enough for one day and made his way back home.

The following day Tommy was up earlier than usual. He had an interview later that morning at the local job centre to check if he was actively seeking work. He had kept a note of each job that he had applied for and also a small pile of rejection letters from companies that had bothered to reply. With a few hours to kill, he wrapped up well and returned to the picket line. He was early enough to catch sight of the double-decker bus turning up the hill towards the factory. This was when the most noise was made and Tommy knew that this was the roar he could hear from his flat each morning. As the bus turned in towards the gates, Tommy could see the scared eyes peering from the windows above and below the large Moffat and Williamson sign that stretched across the middle of the bus. Once the bus was through the gates, the majority of the strikers slowly began to disperse. Some of them would return later in the day to support the diehards who were there most of the day and night. Tommy had a quick stop off at his flat to check on Jade and her growing bump before heading off to the unemployment centre armed with his pile of rejection letters.

The job centre was on two floors and split into different areas. The large reception area had many free-standing notice boards that contained slips of cards with job vacancies and descriptions. If there was a job that was of interest, the person would take note of the reference number and hand it to the receptionist who would then take the person's details and if they were a suitable candidate, they would set up an interview. Tommy gave the boards a quick once over, he had given them a thorough going over previously and from what he could see, there were no new cards on the board. The ones that had appealed to Tommy required experience or a particulate qualification, neither of which Tommy had. For any suitable jobs, Tommy had already applied. He walked over and gave his name to the receptionist.

"If you take a seat someone will see you shortly."

Tommy didn't have to wait long when a scruffy man in his mid-thirties appeared in front of him.

"Tommy Ross."

Tommy nodded.

"Hi, I'm George, if you could follow me please"

Tommy was led through the long office floor to a desk at the far wall.

"Take a seat and I'll check some of your details on here. I see you've come prepared" George nodded at Tommy's letters.

"Yeah, I would have had more but some of them don't even bother to reply."

As George tapped on his computer he turned momentarily and gave Tommy a sympathetic nod before tapping again.

"I see you have ticked the boxes for unskilled, manual labour, manufacturing and construction. Would you also consider hospitality, facilities and property services?"

"I don't know what that entails but if there is a job in that field, I'll take it."

George turned from his computer and smiled "It is mostly unskilled, for example, the facilities and property services include cleaning, refuse collector, and a caretaker, whereas the hospitality industry could be working behind a bar, waiting tables, that sort of thing."

"I'll do it."

"Well there's nothing here at the moment but it means you will now be placed in that category if something does come up. It says your last job was the Timex. You do know they are hiring again."

"Yeah, so I've heard" Tommy smirked.

"Would you consider it? I can put your name forward if you like. There are interviews this afternoon for immediate start."

"Are you serious?"

"We have the notice to refer anyone with manufacturing on their CV."

"Oh, you are serious? And what if I refuse, will my benefits be stopped?"

"Well no, in this case, if there is a suitable reason…"

"…A suitable reason, those people are out there in the cold, day and night fighting for their jobs, including my mother and you are asking if I will consider working for them?"

Tommy was immediately worked up and ready for any retaliation but George appeared to shrink in his seat, sorry that he even mentioned it.

"Ehm, okay, well I've added facilities and property services to your list and if anything is forthcoming we'll let you know"

George could sense the anger burning behind Tommy's eyes

"Do you need me to show you the way out?" George was silently pleading that Tommy would leave without a scene.

Tommy clutched his rejection letters and made his way out of the building.

On the bus journey home, Tommy was continually going over in his head what had happened at the interview. He knew how desperate people were for work and even those with high morals against Scabs would maybe be pressured into taking a job at the factory. By the time he got off the bus, he had calmed down and started to think about his new job prospects. He couldn't wait to tell Jade about it.

"So what happened at the job centre, any luck?" Jade asked as he entered the flat.

"They've expanded my search categories"

"What the fuck does that mean?"

"More job options, they want me to consider hospitality, and also property services, like a janitor or a caretaker, that kind of thing" Tommy buttered it up by not mentioning that it was cleaning and bar work.

"That sounds good, was there a specific job they were recommending for you?"

"Not at the moment but if any vacancies come up they will automatically put my name forward. Would you believe they asked if I would consider the Timex? He knew it was the last place I had worked and said it was policy to try and fill their vacancies."

"And what did you say?" Jade said sternly.

Tommy picked up the hostility in her tone but took it to be in his favour.

"I thought he was joking at first then I realised he was serious. It's only been a week, the unions are still negotiating and yet they are pressuring people into taking their jobs. If anything they should be supporting the workers by not sending anybody for these interviews."

"So what you're telling me is you turned down a full-time job to stand on a fucking picket line and shout abuse at people who are willing to get off their arse and work for a living?"

"What? Jade you have got to be fucking kidding me. Some of those people have given twenty maybe thirty years of their life to that company including my mother and you're expecting me to go behind her back and take her job?"

"In case you haven't noticed we have a baby due any fucking day now and just like some of those other 'Scabs' as you like to call them, maybe they need a job to feed and clothe their family."

"Jade where the fuck is this coming from? Do you know someone who has taken a job there?"

"No" Jade frowned and had an almost guilty expression.

“Well, you seem to have a very strong opinion about it which has come out of nowhere.”

“Hardly, out of nowhere”

“Well, where is this coming from? Come on, I’d like to know why you think it would be okay for me to go behind my mother’s back and take her job?”

“I never said it like that.”

“Well, what did you say it like? Because it doesn’t matter what way you say it, that’s exactly what it means.”

“No, it doesn’t. If those people, i.e. your mother, don’t want to work there, then some people do and will.”

“Do you not understand? My mother wants to go to work, along with the other three hundred and forty-odd that have all been forced out of their jobs. These Scabs have come in and are now doing their job at a cheaper rate.”

“Don’t call them Scabs, that’s not a nice word.”

“These are not very nice people. Why don’t you have a walk up to that picket line and you’ll see how arrogant they are towards the people that they have taken their jobs from.”

“Arrogant? No, maybe they’re just proud that they have finally found a job.”

“You’ve known from day one the reasons why they are on strike and never said anything but now suddenly you have this very personal opinion on them”

“It’s not personal.”

“Well, it’s coming across very fucking personal.”

“Look that’s my opinion, if you don’t like it…”

“If I don’t like it what…?”

With both their voices raised to an intolerable level, Jade decided she'd had enough and stormed away. Tommy walked over to the living room window and opened it for some fresh air to calm down. Minutes later he heard the door to his flat bang shut and watched as Jade hurried down the road away from the block.

It was after midnight when Jade came back in and Tommy was in bed but still awake. He could hear her pulling out the spare cover from the cupboard in the hall, an indication that she was sleeping on the couch. He was tempted to go through and talk to her but he was tired and didn't want it to end in another argument.

It was well after two before Tommy fell asleep but somehow he still woke up early. He crept through to the living room and popped his head around the door to see Jade snoring soundly on the couch. He was still angry at the things she had said to him yesterday and to prove a point he decided he was going to the picket line. He unlocked the front door without any concern of noise as to waking up Jade and marched into the cold air in the direction of the picket line. Before turning the corner onto Harrison Road he could hear the laughing and banter from up ahead. It was a little early for the buses to arrive but a lorry arriving with supplies quickly turned the small pockets of laughter among the strikers to a fierce anger as the loud shouts of 'Scab' filled the air. Tommy saw his mother in the crowd and made his way across the road. He wanted to talk to her privately to let her know what Jade had said to him. He needed to make sense of it. She was tightly packed into the crowd, partly as a show of solidarity and partly to keep warm. Tommy could hardly remember some of their names but they were all smiles when they saw him squeeze through the crowd to reach his mother.

"How did the interview go?"

"Ok" Tommy raised his eyebrows "They asked if I would be interested in taking a job back here."

"I hope you told them where to go." Said one of the women in earshot

"I think I may have overdone it a bit but they got the message."

"Good for you."

A few others close by began discussing the local government's stance on pushing the unemployed to take Scab jobs, all the while declaring in the press that they are backing the strikers and helping with the negotiations to get their jobs back. While they were distracted by their conversation, Tommy took the chance to tell his mother the things that Jade had said to him.

"Tommy, come on, she's nearly due, and her emotions must be up and down like a yoyo. She's probably just worried about the baby and with you not working, there's no money coming in. There are not that many jobs on the go, I mean if there were, do you think we would be standing here in the cold fighting for this one?"

"I don't know, I think some of them secretly enjoy this" Tommy nodded towards some of the strikers near the front of the crowd, the ones who appeared to be baying for blood "It just felt like there was more to what she was saying like there's something else she isn't telling me."

The word was being passed back through the crowd that a private car was approaching with its indicator signalling to turn into the factory. Tommy's mother stood on her tiptoes to see down the hill, there was still a moment before the car reached the crowd. She glanced back at her son's anxious expression and reached down to touch his hand.

"Tommy it will be fine, it will all work out I promise. Just go easy on her. She's scared that's all."

Tommy forced a smile. He wasn't convinced.

The strikers surrounded the car as it waited for the security to open the gate and Tommy stared at the Scabs cowering on the back seat and tried to imagine being there, running a gauntlet every morning to get to work. He shook his head as he caught one of them giving the middle finger to the crowd from the rear window, but only once it had passed through the gate, a pathetic show of defiance. Tommy was cold and after skipping breakfast he was also starting to feel hungry, but being in the crowd he felt a sense of togetherness and decided to stay with the crowd for a while longer.

The highlight each morning for the strikers was the Scab bus, and as they waited anxiously on its arrival, Tommy was updated on the new developments. There were now two Scab buses and both had been painted white to hide the Moffat and Williamson advertising. This had been a reaction by the company after a boycott of the local taxi firm Toft Hill, the same company that had delivered the sacking letters to the strikers in the dead of night. The cab operators were struggling for fares as the public were bypassing their cabs on the rank, some taking it upon themselves to spit on their windscreens as they passed. Moffat and Williamson attempted to spread the rumour that Timex had purchased the buses from them to warn off any bad publicity but this was proven to be a lie after some inside information that the license plates MNU186P and MNU189P were still registered to the Fife Company. Moffat and Williamson were no stranger to bad publicity as it is widely known that nearly ten years previously they also bused Scabs over the picket line during the miners' strike in 1984 and had now shamelessly stepped up to take on the Timex job after every other company refused.

When the buses appeared, Tommy clocked the rushed amateur paint job, with parts of the Moffat outline still visible. As they turned in towards the gates, the blacked-out windows now gave the buses a haunting appearance to them. He felt a little angry after waiting around in the cold to witness more of the Scab's smug expressions as they passed through the gates on their way to the assembly lines where he had once worked. Tommy said goodbye to his mother and walked the short distance back to his flat. He entered the living room and Jade was awake, but still lying on the couch. Tommy walked over and knelt beside her and spoke softly.

"Look I know the baby's due and you're worried that there's no money coming in but I'll get a job soon, I promise."

Jade nodded unconvincingly.

"So can we move on from this?"

"That depends. Are you going to spend every day on that bloody picket line?"

"Jade that's not fair. My mother is there, you know I need to support her. You would do the same if it was your mum."

Jade shrugged.

"Jade come on. I don't want to argue with you about this. I've said I'll get a job, I just can't take one up there, okay."

Jade turned her head away from Tommy.

Tommy let out a sigh. He didn't know what else to say then the words of his mother entered his head. He reached for Jade's hand "Everything will be fine, it will all work out, I promise." He gave her hand a light squeeze.

Chapter 6

Tommy knew he had to get a job, and soon. He had some breakfast and headed straight back down to the job centre. Due to his outburst at his meeting yesterday he had left in haste and forgot to check the boards for vacancies under his new category options.

Tommy exited the lift on the second floor and walked into the large office area. Normally he would scan the headings on each board to find the appropriate category but today he decided he would check them all. The first one had several jobs that he would have applied for but the cards stated that the applicant would require certain qualifications or experience to apply, something Tommy was lacking. He moved onto the next board and took note of the only post suitable, suitable in Tommy's terms meant, full training will be given. He eventually reached the board for hospitality and scanned down the cards. 'Waiter/Waitress/Bar Person' these were not the kind of jobs that were high on Tommy's list of chosen careers, but he was desperate. He took note of the reference number and waited in line to talk to the receptionist.

"Ok Thomas, here is the number for the cleaning job, you can use the phone on the desk opposite and leave your details, for the waiter job, I have added your name to the list and a representative from the Swallow Hotel will call you to arrange an interview."

"The Swallow Hotel"

"Yes that's where the job is, is that a problem?"

"No, not at all, I had it in my head that it was some pub in the town."

"The applicant list is open until Friday, we will forward it to them and they will arrange all the interviews. Good luck."

"Yeah, thanks."

Tommy turned towards the table with the phone opposite but someone was using it. It was free to use for job-seeking purposes only. Tommy kept his distance from the table to give them some privacy. As he stood waiting he kept thinking about the Swallow Hotel as it had been a talking point on the picket line lately, it was the same hotel that the Timex boss Peter Hall had been holed up since the strike started. Tommy's mind began to wander to the strike but he was soon interrupted.

"That's me done mate." The person that had been using the phone gestured to Tommy.

"Oh cheers" Tommy sat down and dialled the number from the piece of paper that the receptionist had given him. He let it ring for some time before hanging up and trying again. This time he let it ring for longer but there was still no answer. He hung up and approached the receptionist.

"No one's answering."

"That's the only contact I have, you'll just have to keep on trying."

Tommy turned to see someone else now using the phone and another person waiting in line. He decided to leave it and call the number from home. Tommy walked back through the town towards the bus stop and all he could picture was Peter Hall, the man who was solely responsible for the strike at the Timex and although Tommy had never met him personally, his face had been printed in all the top newspapers to accompany any story associated with the strike.

Peter Hall was first hired by Timex as a consultant only eighteen months before the strike and was soon named president of the company by the owner Fred Olsen. The previous year to Halls's appearance at Timex, two engineering firms under his name had closed with debts amounting to well over half a million pounds. Olsen, knowing of Halls's recent past, still pursued him to run the company and word was now spreading that the whole strike was planned as the owners wanted the factory to close and Hall was the man to get it done.

“Someone called you earlier about a job,” Jade said when Tommy entered his flat.

“What did they say?”

“They said to call them back.”

“Do you know where they were from, like what company?”

“No, they left a number and asked me to pass on a message for you to call them back.”

Tommy walked over and picked up the notepad next to the phone. He looked at the number Jade had scribbled down and placed his hand on the phone receiver but didn’t pick it up.

“Well, are you going to call them or not?”

“Yeah, I’m just going over in my head what I’m going to say” Tommy lied. He was hesitant because he was worried that it was the agency about to offer him the Timex job again and he didn’t want another argument with Jade if he turned it down. He dialled the number.

“Hi, this is Tommy Ross. I’m returning a call about a job vacancy.”

“Hi Tommy, this is Derek from the Swallow Hotel, I see you have recently applied for a position to be part of our bar staff.”

“Yes, that’s right. That was quick. I am just this minute back from the job centre.”

“We are short-staffed and trying to fill the position as soon as possible. When can you be available for an interview?”

“Anytime really”

“Would eleven thirty tomorrow morning be okay?”

“Yes that’s fine, I can make that.”

“Ok, I’ll see you then Thomas.”

Tommy hung up and looked over at Jade.

"I have an interview tomorrow at half eleven at the Swallow Hotel."

"What's the job?"

"Bar staff, serving meals and stuff."

"A barman" Jade smirked.

"It's a job. I thought you would be happy."

"I am happy. I just can't picture you behind a bar."

"I can't believe how quickly they got back to me. I only put my name forward like half an hour ago."

"That's good though."

"I know. I'll need to let my mother know. Do you fancy a walk up to the picket line with me" Tommy smiled.

"Definitely not"

"I don't mean to stand in the crowd, I'll shout her over."

"No" Jade raised her voice, a clear message to Tommy.

The picket line was quiet at this time of day, the majority of the strikers would not appear until closer to finishing time in preparation for the replacement workers' exit at four-thirty. Tommy saw his mother pouring hot cups of tea from a flask for a couple of older women close by. He walked across the road to join them.

"Hi Tommy, do you want one?"

"No, I'm fine, thanks though."

"How is Jade? Are you doing okay?

"Sort of" Tommy gestured with a slight wave of his hand.

“We’re talking” He confirmed “I have an interview tomorrow morning.”

“That’s great. What’s the job?”

“Barman”

Tommy’s mother smiled.”

“What?”

“Nothing, I just can’t picture you behind a bar.”

“That’s exactly what Jade said.”

“What pub is it?”

“It’s the Swallow Hotel.”

Tommy’s mum’s eyes widened and several heads turned in his direction. Tommy knew why.

“They’re not on the blacklist are they?”

“Not that I know of, well not yet anyway.”

“Well I am about to be a father any day now, and I need a job.”

“I know” Tommy’s mum took one hand from her hot cup and crossed her fingers “I hope you get it, son.”

Tommy hung around for a little longer. He enjoyed listening to their banter as they tried to keep themselves amused through the difficult situation they had found themselves in. Tommy had promised Jade he wouldn’t be too long and said his goodbyes but as he made his way from the small crowd, one of the strikers, John, caught up with him. He was not much older than Tommy, possibly early twenty’s. They had been introduced on one of the works nights out and had spoken briefly in the passing.

“Tommy, hold up” John walked faster to catch up with him.

“John, how is it going?”

“Not bad, considering” John tilted his head towards the picket line.

“Yeah, shit situation to be in.”

“I overheard you talking to your mum, good luck with your interview tomorrow.”

“Thanks, it’s appreciated.”

“Let me know how you get on tomorrow.”

“Sure.”

Tommy continued walking. He was taken aback at how friendly some of the strikers could be. He wasn’t fooled though. He knew that come four thirty those friendly faces will all come together to form a baying mob, yelling, snaring and jabbing their fingers to express their feelings of betrayal towards the strike-breakers.

Tommy had woken up earlier than usual. His clothes were already picked out for his interview the night before. This was in preparation for the slight chance that he slept in, which on Tommy’s part, was wishful thinking. As he sat with his coffee watching the TV he could hear the faint roar from the picket line. He wanted to be there, he could picture the cowardly faceless people hiding behind their newspapers being bussed through the gates. He turned the TV up slightly, he didn’t want any hostile thoughts, and he needed to be calm and positive. After another coffee and a quick wash, he put on his new shirt. Jade had surfaced and smiled proudly at Tommy as he looked sharp in his new shirt and tie.

“Good luck” She leaned in and kissed him.

Tommy had to board a bus to Charleston and then walk another mile before crossing a busy roundabout on the boundary between Dundee and Invergowrie to get to the Swallow Hotel. He walked through the car park to the large glass doors and entered the reception area. Tommy stood for a few seconds and glanced around at the décor. ‘Very posh’ he thought. He had never been in a hotel like this before, the closest Tommy had come to staying in a hotel was a filthy bed and breakfast his parents had booked for their yearly visit to Blackpool.

“Hi, can I help you?” The young girl asked from behind the large reception desk.

“Hi, I’m Tommy Ross, I’m here for an interview about a bar position.”

“Okay, take a seat. Someone will be with you shortly.”

Tommy sat down, he wasn’t nervous but he did have a slight anxious feeling, anxious that if he couldn’t get a simple bar job, what hope was there for him? Where exactly would he go from here?

Moments later, a well-dressed man appeared in front of him.

“Hello, I’m Derek, I’m the assistant manager,” He said softly.

“Hi, I’m Tommy, Tommy Ross.”

“Hi Tommy, if you can follow me please”

There was a small office not far from the reception desk and Derek asked Tommy to take a seat.

“Would you like some coffee?”

“No, no thank you” Tommy was taken aback at this. He had never heard of being offered coffee at an interview.

“Sorry, I am new to this. The manager is off sick and I’ve been left in the lurch, I’ve never actually interviewed anyone before.”

“That’s okay” Tommy was unsure how to respond.

“So I know you were sent here by the unemployment office but did they tell you anything about the position?”

“Not really, no.”

“Well, I will give you a layout of the job and then I will explain the shifts and if you have any questions I will try my best to answer them, is that okay?”

“Yeah, sure”

“So the duties involve serving meals at breakfast, lunch and dinner, in between these times there will be coffees and snacks and you will also be required to work the bar in the evening. Have you had any bar experience?”

“None” Tommy gave his head a little shake.

“That’s okay. We have some good experienced staff that will show you the ropes. You won’t be thrown in at the deep end.”

“I’m a fast learner” Tommy tried to sound confident.

“That’s’ good. Now, the shifts, we have several shifts here but the position you have applied for has two. Early and late, the early is from six in the morning until two, and three in the afternoon until eleven. You can swap shifts with other staff if and when needed. There is also an issue with the late shift, if the bar is busy and things are not cleaned up by the end of the shift, we do expect you to work late to clean up for the morning shift starting at six, but you will be paid for the extra time.”

Tommy nodded encouragingly.

“Do you have any questions?”

“Do I have to wear a uniform?”

“We supply shirts with the company logo but we do expect you to wear your own dress trousers and shoes. What you are wearing now would be fine.”

Tommy felt glad of his chosen attire for the interview.

“Do you have any other questions?”

“Do you have a timescale of when you expect the position to be filled?”

“Can you start tomorrow?”

Tommy smiled before realising he was serious “Eh, yeah sure, I can start tomorrow.”

"Great, if you can be here just before three I will introduce you to the other bar staff and get you fitted out with a shirt."

Tommy couldn't believe it. He was smiling politely but inside he wanted to scream with joy. Derek walked him out to the main reception and Tommy kept his composure until he exited through the large glass doors. He turned back to make sure Derek was not still behind him and let out a 'Yes' while clenching his fist. He continued through the car park to the main road and couldn't keep the smile from his face. He was soon walking faster as he wanted to get home and tell Jade the good news.

Chapter 7

Friday 19th February

Tommy turned up for his first shift half an hour early and Derek guided him through to the bar to show him around. Tommy nodded politely and tried his best to take in as much information as possible. Derek introduced him to Frankie.

"Frankie this Tommy, can you show him the ropes?"

Frankie put out his hand for Tommy to shake "Hi Tommy, have you worked a bar before?"

"No, I've never even been behind a bar."

"That's okay. It's a doddle, you'll pick it up easy enough."

"Tommy, I will leave you in Frankie's capable hands, if you have any issues come and see me and if I can, I will sort it out for you."

"Okay, thanks."

Frankie waited until Derek was out of earshot "It's okay Tommy, you can drop the act, you've got the job now, and don't listen to a word that big poof tells you, he's a useless cunt and will do absolutely fuck all to help you."

Tommy laughed.

"First bit of advice, keep any tips you are given, there will be plenty, and no matter what other staff say about sharing them, tell them to fucking do one, they're yours, put them straight in your fucking pocket."

Tommy smiled. He was going to enjoy working here.

The first half of Tommy's shift was hard work, he was on his feet back and forward from the kitchen serving meals. It began to quieten down around eight o'clock when the kitchen closed and the rest of his shift was easy-going as he was mostly wiping tables and serving the occasional drink or late coffee.

For the first time in Tommy's life, he was now sleeping until late morning. He was not gaining any extra hours of sleep as he was not getting to his bed until the early hours. Having now worked five late shifts in a row, and as it was his day off, Jade left him to sleep as she had already planned her day to meet her friends and go shopping for baby essentials. No sooner had Jade left the flat but Tommy was up, dressed, and on his way to the picket line. He had passed it on his way to work each day but was always in a rush to even stop and say hello. When he reached the factory gates, his mother wasn't there, but as always, he was welcomed into the crowd with a few pats on the back congratulating him on his new job, including John, who worked his way through the crowd to talk to him.

"Tommy" He nodded "How's the new job going?"

"It's okay. It's a job" Tommy made a face.

"Have you seen that fat cunt Hall yet?"

"No. Not yet."

"I know you've just started but is there a way you would be able to get some info on him?"

"What kind of info?"

John's eyes darted around him to see who was in earshot "His room number, who he meets up with, any appointment details, that sort of thing."

"I'm already on it" Tommy winked.

John smiled "I think you need to meet up with us for a proper conversation."

"Who is 'us'?"

"A few of the lads, well it's more like a team."

"A team, like a football team"

"Yeah, kind of, well, we do play football, amongst other things."

"What kind of things?"

"Do you need an explanation?"

"Not really, I'm in"

They both smiled.

"We're meeting up tomorrow tonight for a little adventure, why don't you come along?"

"Adventure"

"Well sabotage is probably a more appropriate word but it's kind of fun so I'll stick with adventure."

"Tomorrow may be a problem, I'm on a late shift again until eleven, and I might not get away until nearer twelve."

"That's perfect for us."

"Okay cool. I'll see you then."

The following night Tommy started to feel a little anxious towards the end of his shift. He didn't know what John and his friends had planned but he was excited to tag along. He walked outside and looked around the car park but couldn't see anybody waiting. He zipped up his jacket and began to walk towards the exit, and then he noticed the lights flash on a car at the far end of the car park. Tommy walked towards it and as he got closer the engine started.

"Get in the back Tommy" John's voice called from the driver's window.

"How's it going?"

"Yeah not bad, the shift went pretty quick. I got a few decent tips from some rich assholes."

"Tommy this is Ronnie" John nodded towards the passenger seat "And that's Archie."

Tommy nodded in the darkness.

"So still no sign of that fat fuck yet?"

"Not yet. I don't want to ask any questions, I'm kind of biding my time until one of the staff mentions him."

"Exactly, as soon as you mention him and anything happens they'll be right onto you."

"So what's the plan tonight?"

"It's a quick job but if it is done right, it could cause a major disruption tomorrow" Ronnie said as he held up two sealant guns containing tubes of strong glue.

John drove up Harrison Road and parked further up from the gates. The four of them exited John's car and casually walked down towards the picket line. Recently, the strikers had acquired an old caravan which they had now parked firmly by the side of the gates. On arrival, three of the strikers were huddled together around an old oil drum with low flames flickering from the top.

"How is the nightshift going then lads" John joked.

"There was meant to be a few others coming, they might turn up, but it's still early. What are you lot up to?"

"Nothing much, we were just passing and thought we would stop and say hello."

"Yeah right, what are you lot really up to?"

"Honest. We were just passing" John gave him a wink.

Ronnie and Archie walked off towards the bottom gates as planned while John and Tommy shifted slowly towards the two main gates.

John peered through the gaps in the metal slats to check on the security guards, he could see the light on in the security box but only one of them was there.

"The other one must be doing his rounds."

"Or he could just be away for a piss."

"Either or, we will need to be quick. Keep your eyes peeled."

While Tommy kept watch on the security box, John pulled out the sealant gun and placed the nozzle into the lock. He pulled tight on the trigger until the sealant filled the lock. He placed the sealant gun back inside his jacket and both of them shifted back closer to the burning oil drum. When Ronnie and Archie appeared from the bottom gate, the four of them said their goodbyes to the strikers and walked towards John's car. Tommy didn't get in.

"Do you want a lift?"

"I'm only two minutes up the road."

"Will you be up here in the morning Tommy?"

"I don't think so. I'm on a late shift again tomorrow."

"You'll miss the morning's chaos."

"I know but I'm sure I'll hear all about it."

"We'll catch up another night."

"Okay lads, catch you all later."

In the short time it took Tommy to walk to his flat, he had talked himself into getting up early to see the reaction on the picket line. Jade was sleeping when he got in and he hesitantly set his alarm before getting in bed beside her.

When Tommy's alarm sounded he rose quickly to turn it off and lay for a few minutes to make sure Jade was still asleep. He crept slowly out of bed and made his way up to the picket line. There were already several cars lined up along the road outside the gates when

Tommy approached and the early morning strikers that surrounded them were screaming into their windows. One of the cars in the long line decided not to wait and drove onto the oncoming lane to overtake the waiting cars before disappearing at the top of the road. Tommy spotted John in the crowd and they both broke into a smile. With more traffic queueing down the hill, the police on the scene were in a heated discussion with the security, and with no other option, they began to direct the Scab cars away from the gates. A roadblock was set up at the bottom of the hill and all the vehicles were diverted away from the area until the gates could be opened. The two buses were already on route and were held up for over an hour until the gates could be opened. The crowd, which had grown considerably in size, hurled their tirade of abuse at the long convoy of vehicles as they slowly passed through the gates. As the last of the traffic started to clear, Tommy caught up with John before he headed home.

"Give me a shout for your next adventure. Whatever it is, I'm in."

"Good man" John gave Tommy a gentle pat on the back as he walked off.

Tommy crept back into the flat and was relieved that Jade was still asleep. Although he was not working that night, he was on early the following day which meant that he would be up at five for his 6 a.m. start. He made himself some tea and toast and sat down in front of the TV.

The national news came on and Tommy was surprised that the strike was not mentioned. He was only twelve years old during the miner's strike in eighty-four but Tommy remembered it being all over the TV and the front pages of every newspaper. It wasn't until the local news segment where they transferred the broadcast to a different studio that the Timex was mentioned, it was a short unimportant announcement with no accompanying interviews, except a rerun of a Politian spouting from a rehearsed speech that discussions were ongoing with the Timex bosses and they were hopeful that they could get the workers back in.

Tommy had listened previously to the Union reps talk on the picket line and he wondered why the politician was being interviewed, he could talk up his false promises and make out as though he is all for the workers but in reality there was nothing he could say or do that was going to persuade the company to change their minds. Tommy heard Jade come out of the bedroom and changed the channel.

The following morning Tommy's alarm sounded at 5 a.m. and he quickly switched it off before curling back under the covers. The flat was always cold first thing in the morning, there was no timer on the heating but as soon as it was turned on the hot air circulated immediately. Tommy sat close to the air vent while waiting on the kettle to boil, as he poured his coffee he stared out of the kitchen window at the thick white frost on the street below, it was at this scene he decided to get a taxi to work. His tips would cover the cost.

It was his first early start on the job and although the bar was closed at that time of the morning he was busy serving breakfasts and coffees. It was a constant flow of guests until around nine when things started to slow down.

"I'm away to nip out the back for a fag break Tommy, will you be okay here for now?" Frankie asked.

"Yeah of course" Tommy continued clearing a table and as he passed a tray of dirty dishes through to the kitchen, one of the kitchen porters handed him a full tray.

"Take this out to table three."

"But there are no guests left."

"Yeah, I know. You need to go through to the fitness suite, and tell the staff on duty to inform Mr Hall that his breakfast is ready."

Tommy looked down at the tray. It contained two plates with metal domes that covered the food. Tommy walked off with the tray but was called back by the kitchen porter.

"Oh yeah Tommy, he takes coffee with that but do not serve it until he is in his seat, he likes it to be hot when he eats his food."

Tommy placed the tray down at table three and set out the covered plates next to the cutlery wrapped in a napkin. He walked through the hotel and entered the fitness suite. There was a large desk by the door where one of the attendants was on duty. From where Tommy stood he had a view of the small pool, beyond this, he could see the windows to another room containing the gym equipment. Tommy glanced up and could see a large man on the treadmill facing the window but it wasn't Hall.

"Hi, I've been sent through from the bar to pass on a message to Mr Hall."

"For his breakfast"

"Yeah"

"Ok, I'll let him know."

The attendant walked over to the edge of the pool "Mr Hall."

Tommy saw the back of Hall's head by the side of the pool

"Mr Hall" The attendant repeated. The head turned briefly. "That's your breakfast ready."

Tommy waited by the door and watched as the man swam to the ladder and began ascending out of the water. As he grasped the top of the ladder and pulled himself up to land one foot on the poolside. He turned to face the lifeguard and Tommy froze, it was him, it was Peter Hall, the man who had caused so much turmoil and heartache to many families and ruined so many lives. Tommy stepped back further out of the door when he caught Hall snapping his fingers at the lifeguard to pass him his towel. Tommy couldn't believe what he was seeing. The lifeguard reached for the towel and hurriedly held it open to help Hall wrap it around his fat barrel-shaped body.

Tommy left the fitness suite and walked back to the bar to continue clearing the rest of the tables. He was anxiously checking the doorway waiting on Hall to appear. It was only after Tommy's second trip to the kitchen that he returned to see Hall sitting at table three, still wearing his bathrobe and slippers. He was picking through the two plates of food as though checking it over. Tommy wasn't sure if he had seen him until, without lifting his head, he snapped his fingers. Tommy was immediately riled and purposefully ignored him by continuing to wipe down the tables. He snapped several more times and Tommy momentarily glanced over and carried on cleaning.

"Excuse me."

Tommy lifted his head and looked over "Yes, can I help you?"

"I'll have my coffee now."

"Okay," Tommy walked behind the bar.

During Tommy's evening shift, he had served many coffees but had only actually used the machine twice and both times were under Frankie's supervision. He stood in front of the large machine and slowly made the fresh coffee. As the froth gathered towards the top of the cup, the thought of spitting in it crossed his mind until he turned his head slightly to see Hall staring in his direction. Tommy placed the cup on a saucer and took it to Hall who was now watching his every move.

"You're new here aren't you?"

"Yeah, I only started on…"

"…Well if you want to keep this job I suggest you learn how to make my coffee quicker."

"This is my first early shift, I've been…" Tommy tried to explain but was brushed off by Hall with a hand gesture to leave him alone.

Tommy returned to the bar to see Frankie in the doorway of the kitchen with the chef and the kitchen porters making a face. Frankie put his finger to his lips and nodded for him to follow him into the kitchen.

"You fucking arseholes, you set me up" Tommy smiled.

"We thought you handled that well."

"What's his fucking problem?"

"He's an arrogant prick, don't let it bother you."

"Bother me, the cunts wanting to have me fired if his coffee isn't on his table quick enough."

"I wouldn't worry about it. Our boss knows what he's like. He's already put a complaint in about almost every member of staff. He's also complained about the food, too much chlorine in the pool, the maids, you name it."

"Why don't they tell him to fuck off?"

"Because Timex is paying the bill, and it's a big fucking bill."

They overheard the snapping of fingers …" Excuse me"…

Frankie saw the look on Tommy's face. "It's okay, I'll deal with it."

Tommy had read and listened to Hall's comments towards the strikers and his lack of respect in dealing with union officials and until this moment he always thought that maybe it was all a front, that to deal with this every day he put on a hard business personality but inside he was a decent human, he never imagined someone could be so callous and vindictive to bully an eighteen-year-old by threatening him with his job over his coffee not being made quickly enough, it told Tommy everything he needed to know.

Chapter 8

Tommy exited the Hotel after his shift and decided to walk home, his head was filled with angry thoughts of Hall and he needed the fresh air. It was only two and half miles to his flat and with the bright sun breaking through the clouds, it was lifting his mood. The time passed quickly and he was soon at the foot of Harrison Road. As he ascended the hill, he could hear the noise coming from the picket line, someone was talking through a loudspeaker and he could hear cheering and clapping. Further up the hill, he could see the large crowd on the opposite side of the road to the picket line. Tommy stood on the grassy mound by the trees to see over the crowd. There was more chatter by the man on the speaker and then more clapping. Tommy recognised the speaker as part of the union. He had given regular interviews and updates on the news about the discussions with the management. 'With the smiles on the faces of the crowd, he must be delivering some good news' He thought.

"Hey Tommy" Archie, one of the Team members stood next to Tommy on the grassy mound.

"Hey, what's happening?"

"The union have announced plans for a demonstration march to take place in three weeks. They are expecting a turnout of thousands."

"Is that it? I saw the happy faces and thought everyone was getting their jobs back."

"Tommy I'll be honest with you. We are never getting our jobs back. But we will make it extremely difficult for them to continue without us. If this place doesn't shut down, this will go on for years."

"Years" Tommy smiled.

"Don't you remember the Miners' strike?"

"I remember parts of it on TV. I vaguely remember the Police on horseback and a lot of fighting. I was only about ten at the time. Was there not a guy with a bad comb-over?"

"Arthur Scargill"

"Yeah, I remember him."

"That went on for a year, there were riots, and a couple of people were killed."

Tommy looked down at the factory gates, and at the row of women lined up in front of the old caravan chatting with their mugs of tea. "It's hardly on par with the Miners' strike" Tommy smirked.

"Laugh now, but you mark my words. This is going to go on for a long time."

Tommy hung around a little longer than expected and once the buses exited the gates, he hurried home to Jade.

"I thought you finished at two?"

"I did."

"Well, where the fuck have you been, or need I ask?"

"Well I would have had to get two buses to get home so I decided to walk instead. I passed the gates on the way and I kind of got caught up in the moment."

"And you never thought for one minute that I would be sitting here waiting on you? Is this what it's going to be like when the baby is here?"

"Don't be daft."

"Well, it's due, very fucking soon."

"I know this. Look I'm sorry, okay."

Jade sat down and slumped into the chair "I just don't like you going there."

“I know, but we’ve been over this. My mum’s there and I like to go to show my support. It’s not as if I’m there every day.”

Jade slumped further in the seat.

“Are you okay?”

“I don’t feel too good.”

“Can I get you anything?”

“No, I’m fine. I need to go and lie down.”

Tommy helped Jade through to the bedroom. He felt guilty now that he had been to the picket line. He made a promise to himself that he would avoid going near it for a while.

Saturday 20th February

Tommy was on the early shift, and again, he was sent through to the fitness suite.

“Mr Hall,” The pool attendant said.

Tommy nodded.

“I’ll let him know.”

Tommy didn’t wait around. He marched straight back to the bar and picked out a cup he had prepared earlier and placed it next to the coffee machine. When Hall appeared, Tommy stopped what he was doing and enthusiastically delivered Hall's coffee mixed with plenty of Tommy’s phlegm.

With not so much as a thank you or even a smile, he brushed Tommy away with a flick of his hand. Tommy continued wiping down the vacant tables and felt pleased each time he saw Hall take a sip of his coffee.

When Tommy finished his shift he spotted John's car parked at the far end of the car park. Archie and Ronnie were also there.

"Hall left late this morning, he's not been back today."

"We're not here for Hall, well, not yet anyway" John joked.

"Come on, I'll give you a lift."

Once Tommy was in the back, Ronnie handed him a sheet of paper. Tommy gave it the once over and saw that it was a list of names and addresses.

"Whose addresses are these?"

"Scabs"

"Really, where did you get them?"

"It's the ones we know, some of them we used to work with."

"What are you planning on doing?"

"Nothing yet, we wanted to know if you wanted in on it when we do?"

"Of course, I'm off tomorrow and then I have another early shift on Monday, after that, I switch back to the late shift."

"What time do you start Monday?"

"Six"

"That would work" Ronnie nodded to John.

"We could pick you up at five."

"As long as I am at work for six"

John stopped on the main road near Tommy's block on Rosemount Road.

"See you at five Tommy"

"See you at five lads" Tommy smiled.

Tommy stood for a few seconds and watched them drive off.

Monday 22nd February

Tommy was up a little earlier than usual to make sure he had cereal before his exploit with the Team. He sat by the window with his cup of tea to watch for John's car but as the minutes ticked by, Tommy was becoming impatient. He had almost given up hope of them turning up when John's car appeared at ten past. Tommy left the flat and hurried down to the car. When he got in the back opposite Archie he noticed a box wedged between them.

"What's all this?"

"Tools for the job" Archie winked.

Tommy peered inside and spotted a large funnel placed on top of a few other objects but it was too dark to work out what else was in there.

"So where's the first stop?"

"It's not too far" Said John.

They drove to the top of Rosemount and continued on the same road where it met with Dalmahoy Drive then up the hill to Laird Street. John turned in by The Nine Maidens pub and then onto Brackens Road. He pulled over at the opening of a small cul de sac and stopped the car. The interior light went on and Archie began handing out objects from the box. Tommy was given a bag of sugar.

"What the fuck is this for?"

"To mix with the petrol" Archie held up the funnel.

John looked back at Archie "Remember and put the cap back on so they don't suspect anything. We need them to start the car so that the sugar works its way through the engine."

Archie got out of the car and led the way with Tommy and Ronnie close behind. He stopped at a car which was parked further up from the closest driveway.

"Why is it parked here and not on the driveway"

"It's his girlfriend's house."

"How did you know he would here?"

"John followed him last night."

Tommy smiled.

Archie removed the petrol cap and held the funnel in place while Tommy carefully poured in the bag of sugar. Ronnie went around the car with a can of spray paint and even in the darkness Tommy could make out the wards Scab across the bonnet. They hurried back to John and drove off to the next planned address. Due to the bright street lights, John had to park a fair distance from the next intended target. Tommy was handed another bag of sugar and as the three of them walked along the pavement, they saw lights from another car.

"Quick get down" Whispered Archie.

The three of them ducked behind a small van that was parked closest to them and waited until the car passed.

"We've not done anything yet. Why are we hiding?" asked Ronnie.

"Well it is kind of suspicious if someone sees three guys creeping about at half five in the morning and if whoever is driving recognises any of our faces they'll put two and two together and know we did what we are about to do.

"Good point."

The spray job was near identical to the last car and once the last of the sugar was emptied into the tank they hurried back to John who drove in the direction they had come from.

"Where are you going, John?"

"I just want to see it."

John drove passed the freshly painted car "Good job lads."

"Where to now"

"That's it for today Tommy, let's get you to work."

John drove to the Swallow Hotel and pulled up at the edge of the car park.

"Same time tomorrow Tommy."

"I can't, I'm on late from tomorrow."

"Oh, that's right. Well, we'll maybe organise a late one."

"Catch you later lads" Tommy stepped out of the car.

"Oh Tommy, see if you can get something on Hall, even a room number."

"Already on it"

"Good lad"

Tommy walked through the entrance of the hotel with a spring in his step. He had a strange happy feeling as though he was part of something. That same strange feeling returned several hours later when he witnessed Hall gulp down his coffee with an added mixture of cloudy phlegm. The rest of Tommy's morning was filled with more devious thoughts to implement on Hall.

Chapter 9

Tommy was on his third late shift in a row and due to the change in hours he had been sleeping late and going straight to work. This suited Jade as it gave her peace of mind that Tommy was not going near the picket line. With the baby due any day and a regular wage coming in, she appeared to be happy. After his shift, Tommy walked out of the hotel and spotted a car parked by the edge of the car park, the driver flashed the lights to let him know it was John.

"How is going lads?" Tommy asked as he got in the car.

"All good, we've not seen you up at the picket line lately"

"Yeah, I know. I've mostly been on late shifts so my sleeping pattern is a bit messed up."

"We have a job planned. It's got to be done early though. We're thinking Wednesday, can you make it?"

"I can't Wednesday lads. I'm on a late shift again, there's no way I'll get up after a late shift. I'm off on Thursday though if that's any good?"

John turned to Ronnie who shrugged back at him "Thursday it is then."

"What's the job?"

"I don't want to get into it just now but the timing has to be perfect. We also have a big plan for Hall if we can get an exact date and time for him to leave the hotel."

Tommy was intrigued "Speaking about Hall, he came in for a late dinner the other night and I managed to put some shit in his food before any of the staff noticed."

Ronnie laughed “What did you put in it?”

“Shit.”

“Yeah, you said, what do you mean by shit?”

“Like, shit” Tommy was confused that Ronnie didn’t understand.

“You mean like real shit, from your arse shit.”

“Like real shit, shit”

“Fucking hell Tommy, how did you manage that?”

“Well, I saw him come in kind of late and speak to my manager, who in turn, walked straight to the kitchen to have a word with the chef. I knew he was requesting food even though it was well after the meals were finished. It’s ridiculous, any other customer would be told to piss off but Hall, oh no, that’s a different story. He is hated by all the staff so I reckon the only reason they tolerate him is because Timex are paying them fucking fortune.”

“And the shit”

“Oh yeah” Tommy laughed “I was needing a shit anyway so I went straight to the toilet but I picked up a teaspoon and a couple of napkins from the side of the bar and I scooped some from the pan onto the spoon and wrapped it in the napkins. In between collecting his meal from the kitchen and walking through the bar to his table, I stirred the shit into his ravioli. Job done”

“And he never noticed?”

“He ate the fucking lot.”

The lads looked at each other in disbelief before they all laughed nervously.

“Tommy that is fucking disgusting, brilliant, but fucking disgusting”

“I’m just waiting on him ordering the pea soup” Tommy giggled.

"Just don't go getting sacked. We have a big plan for him and we need you on board."

"Don't worry. I'll stick to spitting in his coffee for now."

Thursday 4th March

Tommy was exhausted after his late shift on Wednesday which carried on until after midnight. His taxi was waiting outside and he planned to go straight to bed but Jade was still up when he arrived home. She was in a lot of pain and was walking about the flat making groaning noises. They called the hospital but the extractions were too far apart to bring her in. Tommy lay on the bed with her and they both fell asleep. Several hours later Tommy was woken again by Jade groaning in pain. The contractions were still too far apart and Jade fell asleep once again, Tommy checked the time, and it was seven o'clock. He saw no point in going back to sleep. If John turned up he would have to wave him on or go down and tell him he couldn't make it. Tommy made himself some tea and sat by the window.

It was not long after seven thirty when John flashed his lights outside. Tommy went to check on Jade and found her fast asleep. He grabbed his jacket and made his way down to the car. Tommy opened the back door to see a stranger in his usual seat.

"Budge up lads, let Tommy in."

Tommy didn't say a word and squeezed into the back

"Tommy this is Wren, we needed a fifth man for this job so we've brought him on board."

"What is the job?"

"You'll see very shortly" John drove passed the picket line and took a left at Faraday Street and stopped a few yards from Harrison Road.

"Why are we stopping? What's the plan?"

"Look ahead" John nodded in front of him.

Tommy leaned forward from the back seat to see four transit vans parked at the side of the road.

"We hired them yesterday. We're going to block both sets of gates."

"I can't drive."

"This is why Wren's here, but we can't see the traffic from up Faraday Street so we need you to stand here and watch through the trees for the buses, as soon as they appear on Cupar Angus Road, give us a signal and we'll take it from there."

"Why don't you do it now?"

"Because the Police will be monitoring the movement of the buses and will keep the crowd back for us to drive right up to the gates."

Tommy got out of the car and watched as John drove up and parked his car close to the transit vans. They all got out and John gave the thumbs up to Tommy before he got into the leading van. Tommy studied the road through the trees in the distance. He only had to wait a few minutes before the white buses came into his view. As soon as they reached the fly-over he gave the signal. John flashed his lights at Tommy and the first of the four vans manoeuvred onto the road. Tommy hurried up the hill and could see the police making a clear path at the entrance in preparation for the buses to enter. As Tommy got closer to the gates, two of the vans sped passed him and stopped side by side in front of the gates. The drivers quickly got out and ran into the thick crowd. Upon looking back down the hill, Tommy could partially see the back of the other two vans parked at the bottom gates. The police were on their radios and frantically trying to get a message to the bus drivers not to ascend the hill but it was too late, they had already turned the corner and were making their way towards the gates. Tommy smiled as the hundreds of pickets surrounded the busses which had come to a halt on Harrison Road. Within minutes they were causing a tailback reaching down to Faraday Street. More police arrived on the scene to keep the strikers away from the buses and a decision was made by the police to move the buses on until the vans could be removed. A loud cheer went up by the strikers as the buses were waved on by the police to clear the road. Tommy smiled to himself before he quickly made his way home to check on Jade.

On arrival back at his flat he noticed the front door was ajar, when he entered, Jade was nowhere to be seen. Then he heard a low knock on the front door.

"Hi, Tommy" It was his neighbour from across the landing.

"Hi"

"Jade is away at the hospital. Her waters broke. She left in an ambulance about ten minutes ago. She asked me to tell you."

"Shit" Tommy ran to the phone and called a taxi. He grabbed some money and ran down the stairs to wait on it.

As he stood pacing on the main road he remembered the ambulance passing him as he stood watching the scene at the gates. He was angry, angry with himself. He tried to think of an explanation that he could give Jade but nothing came to mind. He could say that he nipped out to the shops but Jade would know that the timing was far too convenient. Even if he did have a genuine reason, no matter what he said, she would think he was at the picket line. When the taxi pulled up Tommy informed the driver that he needed to get to the labour suite at the hospital as fast as he could. When the driver took a left onto Harrison Road Tommy felt sick at the thought of the ambulance passing him when he was there. As they drove passed the picket line the vans were still in place and more police were on the scene. Nothing was said by the driver as he concentrated on the road in front of him.

Tommy paid the driver and walked fast through the long corridors towards the maternity suite. Jade's parents were at the reception when he arrived.

"Was your work okay about you leaving?" Jade's father asked.

Tommy nodded. He was confused at the question and it took him a moment to realise that Jade had covered for him. She must have called her parents after she called the ambulance and told them I was at work.

"How is she?"

"We don't know. We only arrived here minutes before you."

A nurse appeared and after a brief identification, Tommy was informed that he was the proud father of a baby boy.

"That was quick. Can I go and see them?"

"Of course"

"I'll take you through first, then I'll come back for the grandparents shortly" She smiled.

Tommy was hesitant before he entered the room. He didn't know how Jade was going to react towards him. He slowly peered around the door to see Jade sitting up in bed with their son in his arms. Jade gave him an encouraging smile and Tommy walked over to the bed.

"Do you want to hold him?" Jade said softly.

"Sure."

The nurse gently picked up their son from Jade's chest and placed him in Tommy's arms.

"Do you have a name?"

Tommy looked over at Jade and they both made a face. They had discussed several names and narrowed them down in the last few weeks. They both had their favourites but it had not been discussed recently.

"You look like you need a moment to talk. I'll just be outside, let me know if you need anything."

When the nurse left the room Tommy looked at Jade and made a sympathetic face before saying "I'm sorry."

“It’s okay. He’s here now. Everything’s fine, we’ll talk about it later.”

Tommy looked down at his son “So what are we going to call him?”

“I still like Liam.”

Tommy smiled “Liam it is then.”

Tommy crouched next to the bed and placed his head gently towards Jade. They both smiled as they looked down at Liam. Tommy passed Liam to Jade and stepped outside of the room. He signalled for Jade's parents to come in.

“How is she?”

“Come and see” He grinned as they followed him into the room “Come and meet your grandson, Little Liam.”

Tommy stood back to give them their moment. He knew he would have plenty of time for himself once they were home.

After both of their parents had come and gone, it gave them some time to talk by themselves.

“Tommy this stops now okay? I understand they are all angry at the way they’ve been treated and I know you want to support your mum, but it stops now, no more. You have a new job, a decent job and you also have a son to care for now.”

Tommy reluctantly agreed that it was time to move on. He liked his new job but if he wanted his son to grow up proud of him, he would have to find something better. He didn’t want to be serving coffee to posh businessmen forever.

It was a long day for both of them at the hospital and even though Jade and Liam were okay, they were recommended to stay in the hospital overnight for observation. Tommy stayed with them until visiting hours were over and vowed to return early the next day to bring his family home, but not before one last visit to the picket line.

When Tommy turned up to the picket line early the next morning the police presence had grown considerably. After their embarrassment of being caught out by the hired vans, they were coming down hard on the strikers and Tommy could feel the tension building as their every move was being scrutinised by the police.

Not too far from the picket line, photos were secretly being taken of certain strikers, the ones making the most noise, before being documented and filed for future use.

Tommy listened as the strikers talked of future marches and planned demonstrations. The talk excited Tommy and he wanted to be part of it. Then he thought about Jade and Liam. They would be home today, his own little family. Once the buses had passed through the gates, Tommy didn't hang around. He gave his mother a wave from across the road and headed home to give the flat a last-minute freshen-up in preparation for the arrival of his son.

Chapter 10

Things had been good between Tommy and Jade for a couple of weeks, no matter what shift he was working, Tommy took his share of the night feeds. The strike was never mentioned but when Tommy was up early feeding Liam he could hear the chanting. He tried to put it out of his mind, even turning the TV up louder to block out the noise but no matter what he did to distract himself, he still felt the urge to be there.

Friday 19th March

Peter Hall tried to go through the courts in an attempt to use the 1984 anti-trade law that had been forced through by then Prime Minister Margaret Thatcher. This was introduced to criminalise workplace organisations and industrial action by restricting the number on the picket line to six at any one time. The Union fought against them at the Court of Session in Edinburgh and argued that their picket line was in fact, a mass meeting and demonstration. The court agreed and refused to ban them from gathering at the gates.

If the banning order had gone through, it would have meant a free for all for the police to stop any crowds of more than six and take action by arresting them. It was a humiliating defeat for both the Timex and the police who were now cooperating with the Timex management and acting as their private security by videoing the picket line and harassing the strikers by bullying them to keep them in line.

Saturday 20th March

The first of many planned demonstrations in support of the strikers was about to take place and Tommy had mentioned to Jade that he would like to attend, he was hit with a wall of silence and the subject never came up again. Coincidently, she had made an appointment around the time that the march was starting and Tommy knew she had done this on purpose to make sure that he would be looking after Liam and not attending the demonstration. The meeting place for the march was on the grass area off Dalmahoy Drive, a five-minute walk from Tommy's flat.

It was getting closer to the march starting and Tommy was on edge, he had Liam ready to go in his pram but the only thing holding him back was Jade. Things had been smooth between them and although she had not specifically said she did not want him to attend, he knew if he turned up with Liam she would not be happy.

The march was planned to leave Dalmahoy Drive, continue onto Rosemount Road and turn right passed the factory down Harrison Road. It would then make its way down Cupar Angus Road to Lochee Road and finish up in the town centre, Tommy wasn't planning on going the whole way but he was determined to show face. The minutes were ticking by and there was still no sign of Jade. Tommy zipped up his jacket and carried Liam in his pram down the stairs. He thought about taking a shortcut through to Turnberry Avenue but there was a chance he would miss them. He walked fast along the pavement until he reached the bend in the road. He found it strange that not one car had passed him. Before he turned the bend he took one last look down towards his block to see if he could catch Jade on her way home. There was still no sign of her so continued around the bend. It was then he realised why no cars had passed him. Lined up on the road ahead of him stood over six thousand people, many were from local workplaces and trade unionists from all over Britain who had come to show solidarity with the strikers. The strike, now entering its eighth week was also starting to attract support from some known faces, and as Tommy got closer he recognised one of these faces, it was Tommy Sheridan, a Glasgow city councillor and one of the highest-profile militant members in Scotland, a man Tommy had admired from afar.

Sheridan was a member of the Scottish militant labour and was the face of a mass non-payment campaign against the community charge in Scotland, more widely known as the poll tax. During the poll tax campaign, he was arrested and given 6 months jail time after being served an order banning him from attending a warrant sale, a legal procedure for debtors to sell belongings to cover the debt, and even from his prison cell he managed to stand in two elections, the Pollock constituency and also the general election.

With many police and cameras in attendance, Tommy decided not to go into the thick of the crowd and stay on the outside closer to the pavement. As the march got underway Tommy walked proudly alongside them with their banners held high as it passed the factory gates. When they reached the bottom of Harrison Road, Tommy stepped to the side and stood and watched the thousands of people pass him before heading back up the hill to his flat. The march continued without a hint of trouble to the city centre where the large crowd listened to various speakers inspiring them to their cause.

Monday 22nd March

Tommy had been up with Liam since 6 am. After his feed, he settled back down and was soon sound asleep. Tommy placed him back in his cot next to Jade who was also sound asleep. He lay on the couch and watched TV. His shift did not start until three so he was hoping to get at least a couple of hours sleep before then. He looked at the clock 7.30 am, he turned down the TV and opened the window slightly. The chanting had not started yet but he could hear the faint voices in the distance and Tommy found himself pacing the room. He opened the window further in the hope of hearing more of what was happening and paced the room once more. He checked in on Liam and Jade and found them both sound asleep. He didn't want to ruin things with Jade and even though he had made a promise to her, he boldly picked up his jacket and left the flat.

It was not yet daylight and with a slight mist in the air it appeared darker than it should have. From the start of Harrison Road Tommy could see the swarm of high visibility jackets and as he got closer he could see the strikers, it was the most he had ever seen on the picket line and now realised why there was such a large police presence lining the street. Tommy stepped off the pavement to cross the road and was ordered back by one of the officers. Seconds later, he watched four officers grab one of the strikers and drag them to the ground, before placing them in handcuffs and marching them off to a waiting meat wagon. Tommy could feel the tension from both sides. He decided to keep his distance and stay put. The last thing he needed was to get arrested when he was meant to be in the flat tending to Liam. Whenever a car appeared to enter the gates the crowd surged forward onto the road and surrounded it before banging on the roof with their fists and shouting abuse. Once the car passed through the gates, the Police, who were struggling to keep control, grouped together and pushed the angry crowd back from the road.

It was now after 8 am and the buses had still not appeared. Tommy worked his way down the pavement on the opposite side and scanned the faces of the strikers as he passed. He had never seen any of these people before and struggled to recognise anyone that he knew, although there was one face that appeared to stand out more than any other and it was not because they were louder than anyone else, or that their hand gestures were any different from those around him. He stood out because in amongst all this chaos, he stood in a calm and relaxed manner. The face was Tommy Sheridan, a man Tommy had come to admire. Tommy was in awe as Sheridan stood in a laid-back, almost smug-like pose. Then Tommy noticed something even more strangely about Sheridan, his view of sight was not directed towards the factory gates or even the on-coming traffic, he was looking straight across where Tommy was standing, in particular an officer that was on the road in front of him. Tommy leaned in closer to the officer and realised that this was no run-of-the-mill copper, this one had pips on his lapel and appeared to be staring straight back at Sheridan. After a few frantic demands on his radio, he directed his officers to the segment of the crowd where Sheridan was standing. As the officers reached towards him, Sheridan smiled and walked willingly, he knew full well that the Police Chief, along with the press, would have taken great pleasure if he had put up any sort of struggle.

Tommy checked his watch, it was well after eight and the buses should have been here by now. The traffic was still flowing up Harrison Road so the Police must have delayed their arrival until they had the crowd under control. Several more strikers were picked out of the crowd and Tommy decided he had seen enough.

The flat was quiet when he entered and he took off his jacket and peered into the bedroom. He smiled, relieved when he saw that Jade and Liam were still asleep. He went to the living room and lay on the couch with the TV on low so as not to disturb them. He was anticipating the local news to see their take on the scene he had just witnessed.

It turned out that sixteen people had been arrested that morning and the crowd managed to stall the busses for over two hours. All those arrested, despite not being guilty of any crime, were handed exclusion orders and banned from going anywhere near the factory.

The strikers now had the overwhelming support of the working class throughout the country, the union offices were being flooded with donations of money, food and even clothing, and there was even a mass nationwide boycott of Timex products, but the media, after originally backing the strikers and highlighting their cause, now appeared to be turning against them. Their main headline was of course Sheridan, and the footage to kick off the story was the police pulling him from the crowd, tightly edited so as not to show him only seconds previously, standing peacefully with the other strikers. Tommy wondered if any of the news would have covered the strike if Sheridan had not been there. On one hand, it had drawn attention to the striker's plight, but on the other, they now had a known 'troublemaker' supporting them and the press had a way to twist the whole story by portraying them all as mindless troublemakers.

Chapter 11

Friday 26th March

Tommy had organised a night out to wet his new baby's head, an old tradition that when a child is born the father celebrates by consuming an alcoholic drink. This is usually an excuse for a drinking spree as friends of the father of the baby join in and that one drink turns into a continuous night of drinking. Tommy invited all of his friends and also some of the older lads from the Timex to his night out. It was arranged in the Old Bank Bar in the city centre, a pub that came recommended due to their relaxed door policy, relaxed by way of the doorman turning a blind eye to people looking slightly underage. This suited Tommy as some of his friends were underage.

The night was going well and although Tommy was continually being handed drinks by his friends, he knew to pace himself. Archie on the other hand, appeared to be well on, and due to him being more chatty than usual, he let slip to Tommy the Team's plans for Hall.

"So if you can keep note of his outgoings, then we can arrange an exact time to kidnap him."

"What do you mean kidnap him?" Tommy laughed.

"Well not exactly kidnap him, we only need to get him in the car and he can wave us through the security gates, once we are in the factory we let him go."

"Then what"

"We have our sit-in. Open our discussions."

"But they'll just send in the police and arrest us."

Archie thought for a minute. “Well, we will keep Hall with us and tell him to tell the security to open the gates and let the rest of the strikers in. As soon as word gets out we will have all 343 workers sitting in that canteen.”

“So this is the reason you needed me on board the Team.”

“Well yeah but…” Archie looked across the pub and squinted at someone exiting the toilet.

“What is it?”

“Nothing, I thought it was someone I knew.”

Tommy tried to look over but the person was blocked by one of the large pillars.

“Anyway, what was I saying...?”

“I’m in” Tommy confirmed.

“What do you mean? You’re in.”

“The kidnapping, I’m in” Tommy smiled.

“Good man.”

Archie stood up and stretched his head to the side. “I’m sure that’s that scab prick…” He mumbled to himself.

“Who is it?” Tommy asked but Archie had already passed another table with his head still stretched to the side.

He quickly came back to Tommy’s table and shouted John and Ronnie over.

“Lads, lads, go and have a look around that pillar and check out who is sitting in the far corner of the pub.”

Tommy was curious and followed them. Once they passed the pillar they stopped in their tracks and Tommy managed to catch a glimpse of a small group of lads in the corner. He clocked one of their faces and recognised him from the Timex. Ronnie took a step forward to walk over but John tugged him back.

"Wait Ronnie, let's get the others first."

They all trudged back to their table and John gathered the rest of the Team.

"Tommy I'm sorry if this is going to interrupt your night out but I worked alongside this prick for years and the last time I saw him he was laughing and waving his wage slip out of his car window at me."

"Interrupt it" Tommy laughed "Liven it up more like. I'll let the others know what's happening."

Tommy gathered his younger friends together to let them know that something was about to kick off as there were scabs in the pub. With most of them having family or friends of family on the picket line, they had been following the strike closely and they all shared the resentment towards the Scab workers.

While they stood discussing their next move, Ronnie suddenly slammed his bottle down on the table in front of them and marched away from the group. The rest of the Team moved fast behind as they zig-zagged through the tables in the direction of the Scabs. Tommy and his friends tailed on behind them. One of the Scabs clocked Ronnie's approach and stood up with a bottle in hand ready to attack, this didn't faze Ronnie in the slightest as he swung a punch to his head, the rest of the Scabs rose to their feet with each of them grabbing their bottle or pint glass to defend themselves.

As the stand-off ensued, a pint glass was thrown in Archie's direction and skimmed an inch passed his head, he, in turn, lifted a stool above his head and launched it in the direction of the Scabs. It quickly turned into a free for all with punches, kicks and glasses being thrown in every direction. The bouncer, who appeared to be working alone, somehow managed to clear everyone involved out of the pub. The brawl continued outside on the street and turned into a running battle between the two groups.

A taxi pulled up in an adjacent street and as one of the Scabs sneaked around the corner and climbed in, John caught up with him before it had a chance to drive off. He dragged him back out of the cab and landed a couple of punches before he joined back into the brawl leaving the Scab knocked out cold on the pavement.

With the melee happening in the centre of town on a mid-Friday night, Tommy knew the police would be on the scene very shortly and decided that jumping in the next passing taxi would be a good idea, as waking up in a cell the next morning would not go down well with Jade. A couple of Tommy's friends shared the same notion and scrambled away from the scene with him. As the cab travelled out of the city centre, Tommy listened to his friend's animated chat about the events only moments earlier, while the whole time his thoughts were filled with the passing comment from a drunken Archie about their kidnapping plan.

Monday 29th March

The Monday mornings always had the strongest turnouts on the picket line and the police were now aware of this as they turned up habitually in their numbers to intimidate the strikers. After witnessing the situation with Sheridan, Tommy now took in the scene differently, he wasn't only watching the strikers. He was watching the police, watching the strikers. Standing in the distance, he knew who was about to be arrested before it happened. They were targeting certain individuals. The more vocal ones seemed to be their prey even though they had not committed any crime. Tommy was questioning their motive, could the arrests possibly be to justify the money being spent on their costly operation to a private company that was losing production? A large group descended late on the picket line and Tommy overheard that their reason for being late was that their coach, which was travelling from Glasgow, was stopped and searched twice before making it to Dundee, another tactic by the police to stall known vocal militants. The support was growing each week and the police were becoming desperate to break the picket line. Special Branch, including plain clothes, were being mobilised throughout Scotland to try and infiltrate the strikers. Tommy vowed that he would step up his late-night and early-morning activities. He had a note of several of the Timex managers' addresses and also some taxi drivers that were part of the Toft Hill Company that were still driving some of the Scabs through the gates each morning. His notebook of days and times of Hall's schedule was starting to take shape and it was only a matter of time before he had an exact pattern worked out so that The Team could seize him.

Tuesday 30th March

John had organised a meeting for The Team and by the time Tommy arrived, they were already discussing the letters from the Union asking the strikers to obey the law. Failure could mean expulsion from the union and their strike benefit would be withdrawn.

"Losing thirty pounds is hardly a threat, I'm sure that's a hidden message for us to continue, but kind of saying, just don't get caught" Archie laughed.

"I somehow don't think that's a 'hidden' message for us Archie, did you read the Union's statement from them? They literally mention an organised Team! They are publicly outing us and putting the blame for all the vandalism and violence towards the Scabs and their property onto us" John said.

"Well we kind of are responsible for a lot of it"

"Don't you understand, if any one of us is caught doing anything from here on in, we will be blamed for all of it?"

"I know, I was joking."

"Speaking of activities, what's the plan tonight?" Tommy asked.

"Tommy, this is not business as usual, this was a meeting to discuss the future of the Team" John snapped.

"Calm down John" Wren said.

"Calm down, you weren't the one sitting in a cell all weekend, and as of yesterday, Myself and Ronnie now have a banning order preventing us from going anywhere near the fucking picket line."

"Maybe we should have sneaked off in a taxi like Tommy" Ronnie winked.

"Yeah well, at least I slept in a comfy bed all weekend, and I'm also still allowed to visit the picket line."

"That's not what your girlfriend says."

"Look lads, seriously, there are other things been happening to the Scabs that's not our doing and I don't know about you guys but I don't fancy getting pulled in for something I've not done."

Tommy kept quiet. He was interested in what they had to say about these other 'incidents.'

"They are pretty frequent. Do you reckon there's another team on the go?" Wren asked.

"Quite possibly, I think it's maybe time that we cooled off for a bit."

"What do you mean? Cool off. The strike is pretty much ongoing" Archie said.

"Lads, the papers are turning against us, when I mean us, I mean the whole strike, and that's not good," Ronnie said. "I'm in agreement with John, I reckon we should cool it for a few weeks, at least until we see how things go."

"What about the plans for Hall?" Tommy enquired.

"Still keep tabs on his routine. Once things cool off we'll make a decision, but for now, I think we should put everything on hold."

They were all in agreement, and although Tommy nodded along with them. He was disappointed with their decision, but he didn't care, he had been enjoying his own little ventures and was going to carry on regardless. His early morning and late night ventures were becoming almost therapeutic to him as a way of venting his frustrations. He had moved on from the spray paint and sugar in the tank to more blatant acts of throwing paint stripper over cars, smashing windows and slashing tyres.

The following morning, after The Teams meet, a certain arrogant Scab whom the Team had previously singled out, and who had been on their list for quite some time, left his house early for work to be met by a lone member of the Team. The assailant was masked up and beat the Scab with a metal pole to the extent that he needed hospital treatment.

Sunday 11th April

Another march had been organised by the Union and this one had the support of some of the major local firms who came together to form a crowd of over 6000, including N.C.R., Levis, Ninewells Hospital, Dundee City Council and many other smaller businesses. Tommy was scheduled for an early shift that day and had left it too late to ask for a swap. Some bosses felt pressured into giving their staff the day off to attend the march in fear of a backlash for not supporting the strike, but due to Hall being a paid guest at the hotel, Tommy could not risk his boss knowing about his connection to the strike as this would show a conflict of interest and put his job in jeopardy.

It was Monday morning and although Tommy was not scheduled for work, he was still up early with Liam. Hearing the faint sounds of the crowd over the TV, and being frustrated over missing the march the day before, he made a decision. He was going to the picket line. He wrapped Liam up tightly in his pram and sneaked out the door quietly without waking up Jade. He found his usual spot across the road from the main gates and timed it perfectly to see the fierce crowd come alive at the sight of the busses as they began ascending the hill. There were a few militants scattered around trying desperately to break the police line and stop the busses from entering through the gates, but they were quickly marched off by the Police.

As soon as they were through the gates, Tommy made his way home and back in front of the TV before Jade woke up. He had spent the rest of his day off doing chores around the flat, while Jade took Liam out to visit her mother, she returned late afternoon to inform him she was going out again to visit friends. Tommy didn't say anything and was happy to have his father and son alone time. Jade returned some hours later and by the look on her face when she walked in the door, Tommy knew that things were about to kick off.

"Were you at the picket line this morning, with our fucking son?"

"Who told you that?"

"Never mind who told me, were you fucking there?"

Tommy thought it best to lie. "No, I was in here. You know I was in here because you were in here too."

"You were seen on the fucking picket line with Liam in his pram."

"No, I wasn't, but I'd like to know who the fuck said I was."

"It's none of your fucking business who told me."

"I'm guessing it is the same person you go to visit when I'm at work" Tommy stared hard to see her reaction.

Jade took a slight gulp and tried to stare back without looking guilty "What are you talking about?"

Tommy knew that something wasn't right between them for a while now and had been putting it to the back of his mind. He had long suspected that Jade had been cheating on him and kept telling himself that he was just being paranoid, but the look she had given him was enough to know the truth. When he had been on a late shift and he called home, she was never in and said that she was at a friend's house as she hated being stuck in the flat on her own with Liam, but when he was on an early shift she would often leave him with Liam to go visiting her 'friends.'

"Where were you tonight?"

"I was with a friend"

"Which friend"

"A friend"

"Tell me which friend"

"I don't need to tell you anything. Do you not trust me or something?"

Tommy walked over to the phone and picked it up. "I'll trust you if you tell me which friend you were with tonight"

"I'm not fucking putting up with this, you paranoid fuck. You need to get a fucking grip of yourself"

Jade stormed through to the bedroom and started packing a bag with nappies and essentials for Liam.

"Where do you think you're going?"

"Well, I'm not fucking staying here putting up with this shit."

Liam was asleep in his cot and Jade quickly scooped him up in her arms and placed him in his pram.

"So you would rather leave than sort this out between us."

"Sort it out." She screamed "Okay, let's sort it out. Tell me the truth. Were you at the picket line with our son this morning?"

Tommy froze. He wasn't sure whether to keep the lie up or admit the truth.

"Okay, I went to the picket line. Now tell me where you were tonight"

"Go fuck yourself" She screamed. "The one fucking place I told you not to go and you sneak out with our son while I am sleeping."

Tommy marched to the door and stood in front of it. He took a deep breath and calmly asked her "So where were you tonight?"

"Get out of my fucking way" She demanded

"Tell me who you were with" Tommy screamed.

"None of your fucking business" She shouted.

Tommy opened the door and Jade stormed passed with Liam in his pram, he stood by the doorway and watched as Jade angrily bumped the pram down the stairs. He didn't want her to leave, he wanted her to stay and tell him nothing was going on. She turned towards the next set of stairs and was out of sight but Tommy stayed by the doorway. He was still in hope that she would turn back and didn't enter his flat until he heard the door to the block of flats slam shut.

Chapter 12

Tommy's exploits started to appear in the local paper and although most of the public had been sympathising with the strikers, some were now turning against them due to the media's misleading headlines labelling them angry militants, while purposefully forgetting to mention they were ordinary people fighting to keep their jobs. Even when politicians used their influence to push more talks between Hall and the Union, the public were claiming that these politicians were hijacking the strike to boost their agenda and would happily back Peter Hall if it meant the public would give them more votes.

A meeting with the Team was called by John and when Tommy arrived they were already in deep discussion.

"Hi Tommy," John said while the others mumbled his name in acknowledgement.

"Lads" Tommy nodded "You all look a bit serious."

"Have a seat Tommy" John gestured with his hand to an empty seat in front of him.

"Sure, what's going on?"

Ronnie passed over The Courier newspaper which had a front-page story about someone's living room window being smashed in the early hours of the morning. Ronnie passed over a copy of the Evening Telegraph dated a few days earlier of someone being beaten by a masked man on their doorstep while leaving for work.

"Was this you?"

"Maybe, maybe not" Tommy smirked.

"Tommy we know it was you."

"How do you know it was me?"

"Well, it's not just a coincidence that every address that has been targeted was on the list that I printed up, so I am assuming you copied it and have been doing all of this yourself"

"Well, I started off doing the same shit that we were all doing but things kind of escalated."

"Tommy, I specifically told you, well, all of you, to lay low until things cooled down. We were not exactly in favour of the Union for doing this. Now it's not only the newspapers against us, we are losing the support of the public as well."

"I don't think that's down to a few smashed windows. And anyway, you smashed their car windows."

"We had a reason behind that, sabotaging their means of transport made them late for work which slowed down factory production. Throwing a brick through someone's living room window does not slow production, they still turn up for work and it justifies the newspapers to say we are a bunch of fucking thugs."

"It wasn't that when you kicked off in the pub and ended up in court."

"They were singled out for specific reasons. They were the ones laughing at us, waving their wage slips in our faces. They got a beating because they provoked us" Ronnie snapped.

"Look, this is not how I imagined things to go when we started this and I'm sorry to say, I think we should abandon the Team" John said solemnly.

"What about Hall? I have worked it out, every little detail" Tommy pulled out his notebook "I narrowed it down to two specific times to do this"

"Tommy we appreciate everything you have done"

"But this is your chance to get into the factory. It has to happen now before he changes his plans."

"I'm sorry Tommy but we've all agreed. It's too risky."

"Tommy If we get done for kidnapping we are all looking at ten years inside? Do you think it's worth that for losing our jobs?" Archie said.

Tommy agreed. Ten years in prison was a long time to be without his son. He knew Jade wouldn't be waiting on him if he went away, and as far as he can tell she can't even wait on him to finish his shift at work.

It is late the following evening and Tommy is putting Liam to bed when he is startled by a hard knock on the door. Jade, as usual, was out visiting 'friends' but if she had forgotten or even lost her key she would know not to knock so loudly in case she woke Liam. Tommy crept to the door and opened it a few inches, enough to peer out to see two men in suits stare back at him.

"Can I help you?" Their firm knock gave Tommy a pre-warning as to who they were.

"Hi, are you Tommy Ross?"

"Yeah, who are you?"

"I'm detective..." Before they announced their name, they both flashed their identification out in front of them.

Tommy opened the door a few more inches "What do you want?"

"I was wondering if we can have a chat with you about some incidents surrounding the strike."

"I've only just put my son down to sleep and I have work tomorrow."

"This won't take long, or if it's not a good time you can make an appointment to come and see us at the station."

Tommy looked them up and down "I guess you'd better come in then."

Tommy walked them through to the living room "So what's this all about?"

"We have received information from a source that you are part of a group or team that has been targeting certain people because they work at Timex."

"Targeting?"

"Assaulting, vandalising their property, that sort of thing."

"When did this happen, I mean, I sometimes start work at six in the morning or if I'm on a late shift I don't get home until eleven or twelve, sometimes even one. I also have a new-born son so if I did these things you've mentioned, when did I fit it in?"

"You work at the Swallow Hotel, right?"

"Yeah"

"Yeah, we did some checking with your work schedule and given the times of these incidents, it is still possible that you were part of the alleged team that carried out these acts."

"What team? Who else is part of this so-called team?"

"We're not obliged to say at this time."

"Well, then I have nothing more to say."

"We also have information that there is a plan by this group to kidnap Mr Peter Hall."

Tommy froze, he knew someone from the team must have talked, he laughed it off quickly "Kidnapping, that's a bit extreme. Listen I wasn't even part of the 340 odd that were sacked, I have another job and a family, so why the hell would I get involved in a bloody kidnapping" Tommy scoffed.

Jade's key turned in the lock and the noise interrupted them.

"What's going on?"

"They are questioning me about some kidnapping" Tommy made a face.

"Are you Mr Ross's partner?"

"I'm Jade yeah."

"If you can confirm some details for us, we'll get out of your way."

"What sort of details?"

"Some times and dates of when Mr Ross leaves for work and returns home"

"Listen I'm up in the early hours to feed our son, I watch him leave for work and I'm up when he comes in from a late shift, we are both exhausted so I don't know when or even why he would be involved in any bloody kidnapping."

"Well, the times and dates are more to coincide with a spate of assaults and vandalism."

"Vandalism, look when Tommy's not at work he's with me or with our son so I think you've got the wrong person here."

The two detectives looked at each other and stood up "Okay, we have a few other lines of enquiry to look at but we'll be in touch if we have any more questions."

Tommy walked them to the door and returned to the living room.

"So what's this about a kidnapping?"

"I don't know."

"Don't lie to me, Tommy. I've just covered for you to the police; I know you've been out doing things."

"I've not been doing anything and anyway, you're one to accuse anyone of lying."

"What's that supposed to mean?"

“All those times you’ve said you were at so and so house, I called them, and you weren’t there.”

“Well, clearly I was there and left to go to another friend’s house.”

“Well their words were ‘No I haven’t seen Jade tonight’ so, you’re full of shit.”

“Don’t change the subject onto me when you’ve been caught out.”

“You’re the one changing the subject and where have I been caught out?”

“Those times you said you were working, I’ve heard you leave the house at 4.30 am when you don’t start until 6 am or you come home at 2 am when you finish at 11 pm.”

“Well maybe that’s the days I can’t get a lift to work and need to get 2 different buses or I’m asked to stay late to clear up.”

“Yeah right, and you say I’m full of shit. Are you still going to tell me you haven’t been going to the picket line?”

“You know I’ve been going to the picket line.”

“Tommy you’re there nearly every fucking day.”

“Hardly”

“Tommy. You were seen.”

“Oh is that right, by whom? Come on tell me who has nothing better to do than go running to you with gossip.”

“None of your business who tells me”

“Yeah, well when it’s my family involved it is my fucking business.”

“Family, that’s a fucking joke. You’re more interested in standing shouting abuse at people for going to work.”

“Yeah, and you’re more interested in sneaking about with someone else while I am at work.”

Jade placed Liam in his pram and left.

“That’s it. Walk away as soon you’re faced with the truth.”

“It’s not the truth, and I’m walking away because I’m not standing here being accused of something I’ve not done.”

Tommy would usually be hurt when Jade walked out but at this point, he was more concerned about who in the Team had gone running to the police. They pursued him to join them so why would they betray him? His head was messed up. He tossed and turned most of the night and wasn’t feeling the best when he turned up for work the next day.

Tommy was busy helping clear up the bar from the lunches when Derek appeared “Tommy, I need to have a word in private.”

“Yeah sure, give me a second” Tommy placed the pile of dishes he had in his arms on the bunker close to the kitchen.

“We’ll go to my office.”

Tommy followed his boss through the bar to his small office near the reception.

“Take a seat, Tommy.”

“I’ve had a visit from the police enquiring about your relationship with one of our guests, Mr Hall.”

“Relationship, I’ve served him coffee.”

“Tommy, they’ve shown me photos of you standing on the picket line.”

“My mother is there, she’s one of the sacked workers.”

“Well I have spoken to our head office for advice as I wasn’t sure how to go about this and they’ve recommended that due to your involvement in the strike, it means that I am going to have to let you go."

"Let me go. You're firing me because I went to visit my mother on the picket line."

"Well, the police are saying that you're a threat to Mr Hall."

"A threat, I serve him coffee. Come on, I cover every shift that I'm asked, I'm never late, I've never had a day off, and there's never been a complaint from any customer or staff."

"Tommy I've questioned the staff and I can confirm everything you've said but the police have said that you are a threat to one of our highest-paying guests and I need to take action."

"But it's all lies."

"Tommy, they had surveillance photos of you on the picket line."

"I've just told you, my mother is on the picket line, I go to show my support."

"Well, they said the threat come from a good source, I mean, think of my position, what if I let it go and something happens to Hall, I've already had a pre-warning and didn't act on it, I would be sacked. I'm sorry Tommy. I promise I will give you a really good reference for your next job."

"I can't believe this" Tommy shook his head.

"Once the strike is over, give me a call and I promise I'll get you started again."

"But I need a job now. I have a baby son to look after."

"I'm sorry Tommy. It's out of my hands."

Tommy went back to the bar to pick up his jacket, he said goodbye to his workmates and walked home. Jade was in the flat when he arrived home.

"What are you doing at home? I thought you had a shift."

“I’ve been let go.”

“What, you’ve lost your job?”

“They said it was a temporary position, the bar wasn’t so busy at the moment so they had to let me go. They will give me a call when the work picks up again” Tommy lied.

“So what are you going to do now?”

“I’m going to have to go down to the benefits office and sign on.”

Jade could tell that Tommy was down and decided not to bring up their fight from last night.

“I’m sure something else will turn up, you got that job easy enough didn’t you.”

Tommy was expecting their row from last night to continue and was taken back at Jade being nice. It was the encouragement he needed.

“You’re right. I’m going to go down now and see what they’ve got.”

Jade put out her arms for Tommy to hug her. It lifted his mood.

Tommy checked the time “If I go now I’ll catch the next bus” What Tommy meant was, if he left now he would have time to visit the picket line.

Chapter 13

With Tommy having no plans the following day, he let Jade have a long lie while he attended to Liam. It was mid-morning when he received a call at home.

"Hi, can I speak with a Tommy Ross please?"

"This is Tommy Ross."

"Hi, this is Mr Foot from The Timex. We understand that you have recently lost your job."

"How did you know that? I only signed on yesterday."

"We are sent all the unemployment records daily as we are struggling to fill our positions so instead of the agency contacting you and then putting you forward, we can contact you directly. We understand that if you take a position back with the company it could cause some awkwardness due to you having a relative on the picket line, but the job is open if you would like to return"

"Well for one thing, that relative is my fucking mother, no wonder you are struggling to fill those positions, maybe if you gave the original workers the pay they are entitled to, you wouldn't be on the phone trying to turn people into scabs to fill those positions. Do you think I'm going to come and work in that factory while my mother stands outside those gates fighting for her job? Are you fucking mental?"

As the phone line went silent Tommy heard the heavy footsteps storming from the bedroom.

"Who the fuck was that"

"The bloody Timex, who the fuck do they think they are calling me to come and work for them."

“I can’t believe you just spoke to someone like that. He’s only doing his job.”

“I know who he is, he was my mother’s line manager, and he knew fine well I wasn’t going to take the job so why even call me, he could have easily skipped my name on the list.”

“But he just offered you a job”

“So” Tommy was confused

“You do know that will go straight back to the unemployment agency that you’ve refused a job and your benefits will be stopped.”

“Don’t be ridiculous, of course they won’t.”

“You could’ve taken the job, and nobody would know, the bus is blacked out, they can’t see who is on it.”

“You seem to know an awful lot about it. What are you not telling me, do you know someone who is Scabbing?”

“Oh piss off. I was only trying to help.”

“Help, it sounds like you only want me out of the way so you can carry on doing whoever it is you are doing.”

“After the other night, are we really back to this again?”

“Well you’ve still not told me where you were”

“Do you know what? You need to get yourself a job for your sanity. You’re fucking paranoid sitting in this flat all morning or whenever it is you appear back from the picket line after listening to those crackpots.”

Tommy had heard enough, he put Liam in his pram and grabbed what he needed for him for the day and left the flat.

The job hunt was proving unsuccessful as there appeared to be hundreds of applicants for every job and for as much as he wanted to be working, he was enjoying being home every day and bonding with his son. He was always on the early morning feeds and although he could hear the shouts from the picket line, he blocked it out of his mind for a few days. One morning he couldn't help himself, while Jade was still asleep he sneaked along to the picket line with Liam in his pram and when he returned, Jade was waiting.

"Are you going to tell me you only nipped out to the shops are you?"

"No"

"The one thing I asked you not to do was go near that fucking picket line."

"What is your problem? You know fine well my mother is up there and if I want to go and visit her on the picket line I will."

"Not with my fucking son you're not."

"He is also my son."

"Your son" Jade made a face "And a great example of a father you're turning out to be."

"What's that supposed to mean?"

"Why did you lose your job?"

"What? You know why."

"Oh, I know why! Because they found out about your little kidnap plan"

"What are you talking about?" Tommy put on a confused expression but was more confused as to how Jade found out. Apart from the Team, he had only mentioned it to a couple of his friends.

Jade went to the bedroom and came through with two holdalls packed with her and Liam's things. She loaded them onto the pram.

"I'll arrange for you to see Liam but if I find out you are on that picket line you'll never fucking see him again."

"So that's it, you're leaving because I went to the picket line?"

“You just don’t get it, do you? I asked you not to go and you still went behind my back and did it anyway. I clearly can’t trust you.”

“I went behind your back” Tommy smirked “You do know that trust works both ways don’t you?”

Jade didn’t reply and backed out of the flat with the pram. Tommy didn’t follow her but could hear the pram being bumped down the stairs. He sat back down and put on the television, he wasn’t too worried. He knew she would be back.

Chapter 14

It was nearly three months since the start of the dispute and both sides were as far apart as ever. The Union was sticking by their negotiation of a reinstatement of all the sacked workers and Peter Hall was quoted as saying that 'the dispute is over and the sacked workers are now ex-workers.' The statutory ninety-day sacking notice was due to expire, so Timex would then be free to rehire some of its sacked workers and could offer them their jobs back on the reduced terms. If this were to happen their sole intention would be to break the unity of the strikers.

A mass meeting was called and the strikers showed their unity by making it clear that no one was going back unless they all went back but also on the same terms and conditions as before the strike. A mass picket was organised to coincide with the date of the ninety days sacking notice.

Monday 17th May

The Union had heard through sources that the Timex, in collaboration with Tayside police, had organised for the scab buses to arrive at 6.30 am, an hour and a half early. In response to this information, the Union discussed with Scottish Militant Labour and other socialists to come together in support to defy The Timex's planned tactics. The Scottish Militants made plans to bus in supporters and called for other groups to follow suit. With only a few phone calls, Militants from all over the country agreed to come in unity to show their support, some as far as London. Once the news leaked that Militants were joining up to show support, the word began to spread.

Jade had been allowing Tommy to see Liam without any hassle, so he had been turning up to the picket line with his hood up and keeping his distance. He hadn't even said hello to anyone due to his distrust as to who was keeping her informed every time he attended.

On entry to Dundee, the police were using their usual tactic of stopping buses to slow down their arrival at the picket line. These buses contained trade unionists and miners who had travelled from all over the country to show their support. Tommy knew before he even left the flat that this was going to be a huge event as it wasn't even six in the morning and he could hear the chants getting louder. By the time he turned up there were already 2000 demonstrators assembled at the gates with hundreds arriving every few minutes. TV cameras were set up at both ends of the street, and photographers were positioned at almost every angle. A lone person was shouting from a megaphone 'The workers united, will never be defeated' and the strong crowd were chanting back the same words. Tommy looked along the grass verges at the rows and rows of strikers packed in on both sides of the factory gates. He could hardly see a familiar face but their expression showed as much passion as any of the sacked workers. These were not only Militants out to further their political agenda but social activists, here for the mistreatment of the strikers.

Tommy kept his distance and stayed across the road, the reporters close by were scribbling every detail while some photographers came prepared with boxes to stand on while others climbed onto nearby fences to hold their cameras high into the air for the perfect picture of the crowd. The police stood with motionless expressions and still saw it as their main duty to protect a dishonest employer's right to break a picket line by hiring scab labour. These officers that were posted to the picket line duty were not your locally friendly officers that dealt with everyday family issues, or traffic violations. No, these were hand-picked to act as a private security force for the Timex Corporation and act forcibly against the strikers, normal people that were now classed as criminals by fighting for their jobs.

In the days building up to this event, Tommy had been expecting a mini-riot to happen, but apart from the crowd chanting a little louder than normal, he wasn't impressed. He edged closer to the photographers to find a high point to view the scene before him and he found a position that he could view further down the hill. It was now after 7.30 am and with the crowd now waiting for over an hour, they were becoming anxious.

Tommy noticed a commotion at the foot of the hill and caught sight of several hi-visibility jackets moving fast in either direction. Moments later, a minibus sped up the hill and turned in towards the bottom gate. Seconds later, two dark figures emerged from the minibus and ran into the trees. The police attempted to chase them but once they reached the thick crowd they quickly blended in. Tommy smiled as it was almost the same setup as the Team's actions only a month previously with the hired vans. This put a stop to any sneaky move by Hall or the police to let the buses in the bottom gate.

It was now closer to 8am and the buses had still not appeared. Tommy was about to give up hope when he saw the police talk frantically into their radios before reinforcement officers come rushing out of the meat wagons parked nearby and aggressively pushed the crowd back onto the grass verges to make a clear path towards the gates. The signal went up by one of the strikers and seconds later, one of the buses turned the corner onto Harrison Road. The excited crowd surged forward and pushed the police back onto the road. Tommy felt as though everything was happening in slow motion as the crowd and the police swayed back and forth. The buses had passed the halfway mark up the hill and with about fifty yards to go until they reached the gates, the thick crowd surged forward once more and broke the police line creating a large gap. The crowd spilt onto the road and ran towards the bus bringing it to a sudden halt. In a well-orchestrated move, the crowd linked arms and positioned themselves into several rows before sitting down behind each other on the ground. Tommy stood, open-mouthed at the scene before him. This was not the work of several disgruntled ex-employees. These were professional activists, helping a cause they believed in. With so many of them huddled together the police had to physically remove them one at a time. Tommy was intrigued and crossed over onto the grass verge by the side of the buses. From his new position he could see the fierce expression on the militant's faces and not one of them seemed to care when they were being dragged away to be arrested for their actions.

With the police occupied trying to clear the bus route, the other strikers surrounded the busses and terrified the scabs by banging on the windows and shouting abuse. Tommy moved closer to the edge of the grass verge and found himself only feet from the blacked-out windows. He could make out the shadows of the scabs with their arms up over their faces and wondered if any of them felt shame that their actions could cause so much disruption. One of the strikers began kicking the side of the bus and Tommy noticed a slight gap appear in the folding doors. The striker that was kicking the bus also noticed the gap and kicked the door to wedge it open further. Tommy was caught up in the moment and propelled himself down the grass verge to aim a powerful kick at the folding doors. As they sprung open his face dropped, the scabs were huddled together on the floor of the bus, their fearful eyes peering out from under their bags and jackets. Tommy locked eyes with one of them and froze. It was Martin, one of his childhood friends, in that split second he realised why Jade knew every time that he had been anywhere near the picket line. He had confided in him about all the things he had been up to and the whole time he had been running to Jade and telling her.

As Tommy stood staring in disbelief, more strikers appeared by his side and began chanting. One of the scabs bravely stood up from the floor and forced the door closed. Tommy walked backwards up the grass verge and along the fence towards the gates. He saw his mother at the edge of the kerb with some of the other women. He worked his way through the crowd and crossed over to reach her but was forcibly pushed into the crowd by one of the officers. Tommy took it personally and was about to step forward again when he was pulled back into the crowd by John who was several rows behind.

"Let them get on with it" He nodded towards the Militants.

"Thanks" Tommy stood beside him, unsure of what to say.

John smiled "It's all about them today" He looked on proud at the carnage in front of him.

It was another ten minutes before the police were able to move the buses the extra fifty yards to get them through the gates. All the while more and more strike supporters were arriving and the police were forced to concede that no more vehicles could go through. The white-collar-staff arriving in cars and taxis and even delivery vans were moved on from the foot of the hill. Tommy took his hood down, he had no reason to hide that he was on the picket line. Jade would know he was there before he even got home. Everything had fallen into place, her backing of the scabs, her arguments with him over his presence on the picket line. What he did not understand was why she had been pushing him to take a job there, knowing that Martin worked there.

Tommy hung around for a little longer as there was nothing for him to rush home to. He stood with his mother, feeling proud as he listened to the speeches by the Union members and Militant leaders. It was after eleven by the time the speeches were finished and the crowd began to dwindle. As the Strikers and Militants congregated together, Tommy overheard some of them mention that they were going to the pub for a drink, and he decided to tag along.

The large group gathered in the Admiral Bar, a short walk from the picket line. Tommy stood close to the bar and listened as the militants from different parts of the country, mingled with the strikers and talked over each other. He loved listening to their stories and was inspired by their organised violence against the authorities. Earlier that morning when the chaos started, one of the few female militants caught Tommy's eye, she was dark-skinned with afro-type hair and appeared to be around Tommy's age. With all that had happened since then, he had not given her a second thought until a seat at a table close to the bar become vacant and he found the same female sitting opposite.

Tommy quietly sipped his drink, he could hear their conversation but his mind was miles away. He couldn't get the thought of Jade and Martin out of his mind. All those times he was working late he now knew she was with him. As quickly as he had finished his drink he was back at the bar for another. The seat was still vacant and as he sat back down his head was filled with violent thoughts towards Martin.

"Are you one of the sacked workers?" The girl with the afro asked him.

"No, but I did work there, I was paid off on Christmas Eve."

"Ooh, that's not good. I'm Nile by the way, I hope you don't mind, I get a bit chatty after a couple of drinks."

"That's okay, I'm happy for the intrusion. I'm Tommy."

"Tommy" Nile put out her hand for Tommy to shake and worked around the table introducing her friends "This is Oliver, Katie and Stevie."

"The last time I saw you two policemen were trying to pull you up from the road while you were linked on the ground in front of the buses."

"You saw that?"

"Yeah, with the amount of press around this morning, I think maybe half of the country will have seen that."

"When they eventually dragged you away I thought for sure you were going to be arrested," Oliver said.

"How did you manage to get away?" Tommy asked.

"I did what I normally do and fluttered my eyelashes while giving them my most innocent voice of 'Oh officer please don't arrest me' …works every time."

"It's a pity that didn't work for Callan," Katie said.

"Who is Callan?"

"He's another of our friends, he got arrested this morning, we don't know what he's been charged with or if he's going to be released."

"I'm sure he'll be out by tomorrow, when are you leaving?"

"It was meant to be straight after the demo this morning but now we're kind of stuck here," Katie said.

"Callan also happens to be our lift home so I'm guessing we'll have to hitchhike back to London" She half-joked.

"Hitchhike? Can you not get a train or a bus?"

"We're kind of a bit short of funds for that."

"That's a long way to travel with no money."

"You think. This whole trip was all down to Callan, he's originally from up this way and I vaguely remember him saying something about it being his patriotic duty or some shit."

Tommy smiled and caught a sneaky grin from Nile.

"How did you get involved with the militants?"

"I was actually on an anti-poll tax march in London and randomly bumped into Callan, he introduced me to this little group. I liked the notion of helping the oppressed and fighting for people's rights and injustices, so here I am."

Tommy was enjoying the company and the thought of leaving them to go back to his empty flat made him feel slightly depressed. He had an idea which was possibly inspired by their earlier chat about helping people, but most definitely due to the effects of the alcohol.

"Maybe you should hang about until tomorrow and see if Callan gets released. I could let you stay at my flat for the night, well, I don't just mean you, I mean all of you, well, not all of you, your group that is waiting on Callan" Tommy gestured to the rest of the table.

"I get you" Nile smiled "That would be great, but we wouldn't want to put you out or anything."

"That's no problem. I'm kind of on my own at the moment" Tommy cringed as soon as the words came out.

Nile frowned but put it to the others. They knew their alternative options did not sound so appealing and immediately took Tommy up on the offer without any further discussion.

The group left the pub and chipped in to buy some cheap alcohol from the local off-licence and Tommy led the way to his flat. He called Bell Street station where Callan would have been taken after he was arrested to find out when he was being released, but they won't give out any information. Tommy left them his number. As the alcohol flowed, the group discussed some of their previous demos and the trouble they had found themselves in. This made Tommy mention some of his ventures and there were a few raised eyebrows about the planned kidnapping but Nile seemed intrigued and urged Tommy to tell her more about it.

It had been a long day and Tommy was struggling to stay awake. He passed through some spare covers and left them in his living room to go to his bed. When he woke in the morning Nile, fully dressed, was curled up next to him. Tommy snuck out of bed and quietly got dressed. He popped his head into the living room and upon seeing them all still asleep, he decided to nip to the shops for some essentials. He picked up a basket and worked his way around the aisles picking up milk, rolls and bacon before heading towards the till, while waiting to be served he scanned the rack of newspapers and his face soon dropped when he read each headline of the red tops, 'Mob demo terror' 'Worst picket line violence since the miners' strike' 'Attempted murder on picket line' Tommy picked up each one and hurried back to the flat. The others were awake when he arrived home.

"We got woken up by your phone," Katie said.

Tommy immediately thought of Jade.

"It was Callan. He's going to be released later, I hope you don't mind, I've given him your address, he has to come back up this way to get his car anyway."

"Yeah, that's okay."

Tommy laid out the newspapers "Look at this."

They all leaned over each other to read the headlines.

"Wow, I can't believe this, it was nothing like that," Stevie said.

"Talk about sensationalism, oh my fucking god" Katie added.

Tommy left them to read the story and went to the kitchen to make them breakfast. Nile followed him through.

"Hi, do you need a hand?"

"That would be great, thanks.

"I hope you didn't mind me sharing your bed last night."

"I don't remember you coming through. What time was it?"

"I'm not sure. It wasn't long after you went through, I was just really cold and there weren't enough covers to go around."

"I wish I'd stayed awake now" Tommy smiled.

"I did say your name but you were out for the count."

"You know the reason why the media are fucking turning on us" Oliver's voice had an angry tone to it "It is to justify the heavy-handed actions of those fucking police yesterday."

"His next point will be that they are all in on it to keep the working man down" Nile whispered to Tommy.

"I swear this was all planned to keep us, the working people down."

Nile and Tommy sniggered from the kitchen.

"I will guarantee you that all those arrested yesterday will be released without charge, this fucking front page news of attempted murder is all bullshit, and it's all a smoke screen for the police to justify their presence. Whether these charges get dropped at a later date doesn't matter, it is for the police to say to the government, look at these hooligans causing trouble, if we weren't there god knows what would have happened, the government will panic and gift them extra funding for the following year."

Tommy and Nile came through with the coffee and both Stevie and Katie gave them a roll of their eyes as Oliver was still scanning the newspapers to pick out stories to fit his agenda.

It is late afternoon when Tommy received a call from Callan, the group's driver. Tommy passed the phone to Stevie.

"Hi Callan, how are you? …So you haven't been charged with anything?" Stevie looked at Oliver. …" What, you're fucking joking? …" A girl had her arm broken yesterday and was taken to the cells straight after the hospital, she has been released with Callan. Also, the two people arrested for attempted murder have been released without charge."

"See, I fucking told you" ranted Oliver.

"Okay, settle down Nostradamus" said Stevie.

"Yeah we are in a flat not too far from the picket line…you're getting dropped off back at your car, okay we'll meet you there" Stevie hung up the phone. "The girl who had her arm broken had a friend pick her up and she is going to drop Callan back at his car. Do any of you remember where he parked it?"

"If we get to the picket line, I know where it is from there," said Katie.

They made their way to Callan's car and Nile and Tommy were several steps behind the others. They both wanted to chat but each time their eyes met they smiled nervously and continued walking. Nile eventually made a move and took hold of Tommy's hand.

"That's Callan's car just up ahead" announced Katie.

Katie's words hit Tommy hard, he knew his happy moment was about to end. Before they reached Callan's car, Nile tugged on Tommy's hand to make him face her, they locked eyes and Tommy placed both arms around her. Nile leaned softly towards Tommy and kissed him.

While the others stood waiting by Callan's car, Nile and Tommy slowly made their way towards them.

"So do you promise to come and visit?"

"Of course"

"And you have my number?"

"I have your number and your address."

"It's just a squat but it should be good for a few weeks. If anything changes I'll keep you updated."

Nile leaned in to give Tommy another kiss but it was cut short by Callan sounding the horn on the car.

Callan put out his hand from the driver's window "Tommy is it?"

Tommy leaned forward to shake it.

"Thanks for taking care of them last night."

"It was no problem. I enjoyed listening to their stories."

"Well if you get a chance to come join us we'll maybe create some of our own stories."

Tommy watched them drive off and Nile blew him a kiss from the back window. Once the car was out of sight, Tommy walked back to his flat. He hesitantly called Jade to arrange to see Liam.

"You've got to be fucking kidding me. You are never going to see Liam again."

Reality had hit home.

Chapter 15

"So what happened to the guys that were arrested for attempted murder, surely they couldn't just drop an attempted murder charge? I mean that's a pretty hefty charge, especially with all those coppers on the picket line as witnesses" asked Liam

"I went for a newspaper the following day and there was no mention of the attempted murder, there was not even a mention of the strike, it was all dropped as though it never happened. The busiest most violent day on the picket line since the strike started and within a day, the whole thing was completely dropped by the media"

"So your new friend Oliver was right, the police bumped up the charges to justify their massive operation."

"Oliver was not a friend" stated Tommy "But yeah, he was definitely onto something. Back then, there were huge cutbacks, vital services were being run down and police budgets were about to be cut. So the Chief constable at the time, Jack Bowman, needed something to justify spending hundreds of thousands of pounds on protecting the profits of a private corporation. The Police, The Unions, The Militants, The Politicians, The Media, they were all using The Timex Strike for their agenda"

"But if their sole intention was to close the factory, why didn't they pay their staff what they were due and then close it, instead of dragging it out like that? It would have saved them a fortune."

"I don't think they wanted to close it, they wanted a non-union factory, a place where they could hire and fire at will, cut the workers down to the bare minimum for maximum output. That was just the start of things though."

"What do you mean?"

“Well it’s now over twenty years later and you have multi-billion pound companies exploiting workers with zero-hour contracts, all with the government's approval. People on benefits are pushed into taking these zero-hour contract jobs, and even though they can go weeks without any hours or pay, they are officially employed. So from the government’s point of view, these companies have done them a favour and brought the employment rate down. They don't give a shit about these people. All that does is tick a box for voters. The Tories are about to introduce the biggest clampdown on unions in thirty years with new plans to criminalise picketing. This will block the flow of union funds to the labour party and attempt to bankrupt them. They are making it appear political but their real goal is to take away any rights to workers and stamp out what little fight they have left.”

“The labour party” Liam made a face “They were supposed to be the party for the people, the working class, they eventually got into power and turned out to be just as bad. Same party, different colour. It doesn't matter which party is in power, nothing changes. No wonder anybody gives a shit about politics anymore."

“What they need is a new workers' party, one that will represent the interests of real working-class people and expose the gap between rich and poor."

“The public would still not get off their arse and vote. Society is different now Dad. Nobody cares about each other, never mind some guy spouting shite about politics.”

“Some guy like me” Tommy smiled and took the hint.

"What happened to the girl, Nile?" Liam asked.

“She kept in touch. She would occasionally write and call whenever she could. She would always ask when I was coming down to visit.”

“Why didn’t you go?”

“I did eventually, but remember, I had a son. After that crazy Monday, right up until the factory closed three months later, I never went near that picket line. I wasn’t getting to see you, but I tried.

Believe me, I fucking tried. Your mother was sticking to her guns. I would call every single day asking if I could see you. I pleaded with her, I pleaded with your grandparents but they wouldn't budge. They wouldn't even bring you to their front door so that I could see you. Then I saw Martin pushing your pram on his own one day, so I marched over, I thought he would be man enough to have a conversation with me and sort things out. Not only had he been sleeping with my girlfriend behind my back but he had run to her every time he saw me on the picket line like a little snake, so to see him taking over the role of pushing your pram, it fucking choked me up, but I thought, I'm going to be the bigger man here and talk this out. Do you know how hard that was for me to rise above that? Stand face to face and plead with him to persuade your mother to let me see my son. Anyway, when I approached him, he started shouting and making a scene, calling me this and that, saying I didn't deserve your mother and that he was going to take care of her, I knew he was trying to provoke me so I walked away."

"I thought you hit him?"

"Not that time. Oh, believe me, I wanted to. I remember turning back around and he had that smug look on his face, then I saw the pram and thought, if I do this, I'm playing right into his hands. He was goading me to hit him."

"So what did you do?"

"I had to walk away?"

"Hearing this makes me want to go and give him a slap right now."

"Yeah well, that same night, I received a visit by the police and was charged with threatening behaviour."

"But nothing happened"

"I know that, he knew that, but the police said there were witnesses. That's the kind of person I was dealing with. Anyway, that was the start of it, whenever I turned up at their house, they called the police. If I called their house, they called the police. I was completely lost, like, really down. I had a few friends stick by me and cut him off.

I even had a few of her friends come up to me and say that they thought what she was doing to me was bang out of order. The only thing I looked forward to back then was the letters and calls from Nile. The strike was dwindling, there were fewer and fewer people attending as most of them, like myself, knew that after the events on the seventeenth of May, there was no going back. Many of them struggled to find jobs and their bills were piling up, some were close to losing their homes. The boycott campaign was having a big effect on the Timex internationally and the strike was a stalemate. There could only be two possible outcomes, the full reinstatement of all the workers or the closing of the factory. Hall was forced to resign as he had been unable to deliver a non-union factory to his bosses in the States. The company conceded and after forty-seven years the factory closed its doors for the last time on the twenty-ninth of August. I vaguely remember a rumour that even the security guard on the site had to find another way to get in."

"Is that when you left for London?"

"Yeah it was around this time, I can't remember the exact days as things were a little blurry. I was at the lowest point I had ever been in my life and I'm sure I was on the verge of turning up at Martin's door and doing some real damage. Then I remember receiving another call from Nile and she knew something was wrong. She mentioned me coming to London again and I thought why not, there was nothing for me here. I couldn't get a job, I had charges pending. I don't know if I was in love but I was drawn to her, I was young and she was practically begging me to come and visit her, so I packed up and left. Six weeks later, I was arrested for murder."

Chapter 16

It had been three months since Tommy was released and he had been happily living in Liam's spare room while helping him several days a week with his mobile car valeting business. Tommy had gone through the system when he was first released, claiming benefits and going through the whole rigmarole with the agency staff and being pushed to find a job. At one of his fortnightly interviews to discuss his job-seeking strategy he witnessed the security escorting one of the claimants out of the building. He had been informed that he was being sanctioned for being late and his benefits would now be cut. The claimant was adamant that they called in advance to change the time due to a hospital appointment but the agency staff had no record of it. The staff had a reputation of being unpleasant but Tommy never had any problems. They always appeared to be overly helpful when they were going over his resume, especially when they came across his murder charge. Tommy was recommended for many jobs, some with guaranteed interviews, but each one followed the same procedure, the interviewees were impressed until his criminal record was discussed.

Tommy knew it was all a waste of time as he was never going to get those jobs, but he had to attend the interview or his benefits would be stopped. Liam could tell that he was frustrated and it took a lot of persuasion to make him sign off and come work for him. Tommy's point was that Liam wasn't busy enough to take someone on, but Liam insisted. It didn't take long for Tommy to work out the calculations of each job was not enough to pay two wages and the extra income was coming from another source, but it was a conversation neither of them was ready to discuss.

Liam was enjoying living, working, and getting to know his father properly after all those years. He liked listening to his advice and was impressed at how knowledgeable he was having been locked up for so long. He especially liked when he could figure out certain people that he had only just met. The only other person he had seen do this was his 'Uncle' Ginge. Ginge wasn't his real Uncle, he was like an older friend that had been in his life, lurking in the background and appearing every so often to check on him. As he got older and found himself in trouble, Ginge was the one who stepped up to guide him. The car valeting business was Liam's idea but with Ginge's contacts it was now a lucrative enterprise, a cash business to launder drug money.

Tommy waited patiently on Liam to start the van so that he could warm his hands up on the heater. They had finished their first job of the day, a mini valet which included an outside power wash and an inside hoover and polish. Liam drove into a site near an old factory warehouse and pulled up close to a row of flashy top-of-the-line cars. The building had been renovated and was now a call centre for a company supplying double glazing. Liam went into the reception and picked up a set of keys. The customer was a regular and when Liam came outside and pressed the button on the keys twice, the lights on a Mercedes car flashed and all the locks opened. Tommy exited the work van and slid open the side door to power up the generator in the back.

"I forgot to say, I saw Ginge last night."

Tommy looked up intently "Yeah, how is he getting on?"

"Still the same, always into something"

"Where did you see him?"

"In the Claverhouse"

"You never mentioned you were going to the pub."

"I was driving passed and saw him outside on his phone. I beeped and waved and he shouted me over. He asked how you were getting on and I mentioned you were working with me."

"What did he say?"

"He said you 'are a wasted talent"

Tommy forced a fake smile

"He told me to tell you that he has a bit of work if you are interested, something about it requiring your expertise."

"Same old Ginge"

Liam knew Tommy was trying to get out of the conversation and he waited a moment to see if he would follow up on 'same old Ginge' but Tommy continued setting up in silence.

Liam eventually pressed him "So what did he mean by your expertise? Is it to help him run the pub or something?"

Tommy looked over at his son. It was a question he was not prepared for. He forced an attempt to soften his chilling expression before quickly confirming "Something like that."

Nothing more was said between them as they worked together cleaning the expensive car. It was a full valet and once it was scrubbed down and hoovered, both of them worked hard to polish it to a high standard. Liam left his new personalised air fresheners on the dashboard, a small touch that made the job look more professional, before handing the keys back into the reception. On the way to the next job, there was still a silence between them and although most of the time they were comfortable in their silence. This was not one of those moments and Liam couldn't leave it alone.

"So what's up with you and Ginge? How do you know each other?"

Tommy turned to face his son. He knew these questions were going to come sooner or later. He took a deep breath and gave him a faint smile "I ran into him inside many years ago."

"You must have been pretty close, I mean, he's been looking out for me basically most of my life."

"We were cellmates for a bit" Tommy stated, hoping this would be the end of the conversation.

Liam nodded as though satisfied with the answer… "But if you were so close, how come you haven't been to see him since you came out?"

"I can't be associated with him."

Liam looked at him for a more depth explanation but when Tommy didn't expand he stared at him in an attempt to force it out of him.

"I can't be in his company because I am on parole and being in Ginge's company would raise suspicion. If we randomly passed in a supermarket and they saw us acknowledge each other it would throw up a red flag."

Ginges' real name is Rodney McNaughton, nicknamed 'Ginge' due to his long swaying red hair. He has a reputation for being part of the football hooligan scene and still enjoys the occasional tussle on the terraces to show that he is still involved in the scene. This is all a front as Ginge has several other criminal interests and in recent years he has moved up the ranks of the local gangster to be a known person of interest in the National Crime Agency which coincidently, all started after leaving a cell he shared with Tommy Ross.

1999

Wednesday 17th November

On the thirteenth of November 1999, the Scotland national football team played their long-time rivals England in a Euro Cup play-off game at Hampden Park. Scotland was beaten after two goals from Paul Scholes and four days later, the return game was like a forgone conclusion. During the build-up to the game, Tommy had overheard several abusive comments about the Scots from his fellow inmates and as he was one of the rare Scots in Brixton prison, the comments could have been directed at him but Tommy had never been a football fan and even if he was, none of the prisoners would have dared single him out for the abuse. There was an atmosphere in the prison during the build-up to the game and Tommy had shown a feigned interest but after Scholes put England ahead he had decided to retreat to reading one of his books. When the second leg was being played, he was busy in his cell when he heard a roar of boos around the prison and he took it that Scotland had scored. With England not even having a shot on target throughout the whole game and Scotland going on to win, it had not bothered him that he had not made the effort to watch, as due to the two goals in the first tie, it was enough to stop Scotland from qualifying and it would be another four years before they could try again for the tournament. They did have the world cup in two years but Tommy did not hold out much hope.

The following morning, the talk in the prison was mostly about which team England would face in their group stage of the tournament. There was also some talk of the violence after the game between the fans. The trouble had resulted in many arrests, so many, that the police cells were packed with supporters from both sides. Most were for minor drunken behaviour but some were for more serious crimes. The police were struggling to control them, and a plea was put out for any empty cells out-with the area to be used for any supporters that had been charged with more serious crimes to await their turn in front of the court.

Days later, Tommy was informed that one of those arrested after the game was to be transferred to Brixton. Coincidentally, he was from Dundee and was going to be on remand in Brixton until trial. Tommy enquired about him and was told his name was Rodney McNaughton but he had never heard of him. It was late in the afternoon when he arrived and Tommy decided to step out of his cell and take a look at the 'new meat' as the other prisoners would say. When the buzzer sounded to open the main gate, a tall well-built lad with long ginger hair down to his shoulders appeared behind one of the screws. With one screw leading the way, Rodney followed on and the first thing Tommy noticed was his swagger. He bounced as he walked and it made his arms swing wide and his hair sway in a rhythm. For a young lad, he had a scowl that Tommy hoped he could back up. There were several boos and hisses from the other prisoners but Rodney appeared to take it in his stride. Tommy went back to his cell and wondered if, after a few days, he would still have the bounce in his step.

In prison, a person with too much confidence can attract as much danger as a person who is timid or insecure as both stood out and in Tommy's experience, anyone that stood out was a target. When Ginge entered the prison, his confidence was like a red rag to a bull. Tommy overheard him talking and picked up on the Dundee accent straight away. He also clocked the rats of the prison eyeing him up, and as he bounced along the gantry sporting his shiny new trainers, Tommy wondered which inmate would be wearing them by the end of the day. He had thought about warning off the rats immediately but as he had been working hard on his appeal, he did not need the distraction of taking a new inmate under his wing or the drama of dealing with the hierarchy, so he decided to keep his distance for the time being and let Ginge find his feet. He did not know his situation but could tell that he was too young to be in here and therefore would be on remand and protected to a certain degree.

It did not take long before Ginge had his first encounter with the prison rats and surprisingly, he handled it well. Tommy could have stepped in but wanted to see how he would react. He took it well and retaliated just as Tommy had done but this had brought more attention to him, attention that Tommy knew would lead to Rodney being hurt. The rats returned, more heavy-handed and Ginge was caught short. Tommy kept an eye on him and clocked his movements. Ginge was circling his prey and Tommy, seeing the trouble Ginge was about to bring, decided to pull him aside.

Tommy did not look like your typical hard man inmate because he wasn't the typical hard man inmate. He didn't bully or talk down to other inmates and was always polite and gave respect, although his reputation was something completely different. He was the prisoner that would go to certain lengths to protect himself that other prisoners would not. If a confrontation occurred, Tommy used his persona to stay cool, smile and back away, he knew not to react as it would either go one of two ways, the instigator would come grovelling once they were informed who Tommy was and what he was capable of or if they kept it up Tommy would take care of them in his way in his own time.

"McNaughton" Tommy nodded for him to come over. "You wouldn't happen to have a relation by the name of Buster?"

“Yeah, he’s my old man. Who are you?”

“I’m Tommy, Tommy Ross."

"Do you know Buster?"

"No, but I'd heard his name a few times growing up."

“Your accent sounds familiar, you from up near my way?”

“Dundee actually”

“No shit. It’s got a very English twang to it.”

“It’s still Scottish to them.”

“Yeah, I’ll bet.”

“Listen I know what you’re planning, I’ve been there and the price for what you are about to do will be a huge debt”

“A debt to whom”

“To someone you don’t want to owe a debt to”

“What if I don’t pay the debt?”

Tommy nodded in the direction of the small group staring in Ginge’s direction “The rats will have free reign to do as they please.”

“What kind of debt?”

“A debt that you can never take away even after it’s paid.”

“You’re saying you’ve been there, you must have settled your debt.”

“It’s a never-ending debt”

“Why are you helping me?”

“I didn’t want to, but it came down to a need or a want” Tommy put his hands up in a weighing gesture.

Ginge gave a peculiar expression.

“Everything in here is a need or a want. If the need outweighs the want, you take it. If it’s equal, then you need to decide if the want is worth the risk. If want outweighs the need, then sometimes you have to let it go.”

“So I was a need.”

“Without question”

“How long have you been in here?”

“I was here for six months on remand, young offenders for two years and then shipped back here four years ago.”

“How long do you have left?”

“A long-time” Confirmed Tommy

Ginge sat next to Tommy during lunch and clocked the rats glaring at him.

“Fucking pricks, I’m going to get every single one of them.”

“They are nothing” Said Tommy “Ignore them.”

“Easy for you to say, they’re not coming after you. It’s all about survival of the fittest right?”

“Survival of the fittest, do you know what that means?”

“Only the strongest survives.”

Tommy shook his head “It’s about adapting to your environment. Do you see that guy at the end of the last row of tables?”

Ginge turned his head slightly to see a huge guy with arms twice as big as the guy next to him.

“He holds the prison record for bench pressing. Those slimy rats would take him out in a second if he had something they wanted.”

Tommy nodded over to the table by the far wall. A small older black man in the middle of the table gave Tommy a nod back. Moments later, someone from the table signalled towards the rats and their heads solemnly turned away from Ginge to be more interested in their food tray.

"What the fuck just happened?"

"When you've finished eating, collect your things from your cell, you're moving."

"Where to"

"Mine."

Ginge looked up at the top table and the small man in the middle gave him a nod. Ginge nervously nodded back.

"Why the fuck is going on?"

"Survival of the fittest" Tommy winked "Adapt" He said sternly.

Over the next few weeks, Tommy explained to Rodney about how the prison system worked. If Tommy had not stepped in and let him continue with his ongoing feud with the other prisoners, no matter who came out on top, Rodney would have had a huge debt to pay, either with his life or like Tommy, he would be forever in someone's debt.

"You have to keep a low profile in here and try not to draw attention to yourself. There is always someone looking for a target, if you make yourself known, you will be the target. Never show your anger or aggression and pick your battles. If you see other shit going on, even if it's right next to you, walk away."

"Why are you helping me?"

"I have a favour"

"What kind of favour?"

"Not now, when you get out."

Chapter 17

The official age of entry to an adult prison is twenty-one but under certain circumstances the law can permit someone to be detained from the age of sixteen, these circumstances include, if the person is on remand and awaiting trial, the crime the person is charged with is extremely violent or any other appropriate youth prison is full. In October 1993, Tommy, only a month shy of nineteen, was remanded in Brixton prison and charged with the murder of a policeman. After Tommy's trial, he was sentenced to a minimum of twenty years. He had spent a year and a half in Feltham Young Offenders Institution and only days after turning twenty-one, Tommy was shipped back to Brixton to finish his sentence. When Tommy was previously in Brixton, he was a teenager on remand and there was an unwritten rule that teenagers or remand prisoners were to be protected unless they were being detained for non-acceptable crimes such as rape, child sex offending or child killing. On his return, he was now classed as an adult and the protection he had previously received, no longer applied, but in respect of his murder charge, he had been left alone by the other prisoners with some even glorifying his charge due to the victim being a policeman, but this brought other problems.

Tommy was an angry young man, angry that he came down to London for an unplanned short trip and was now serving a life sentence. Since arriving back in Brixton prison from Feltham he had been concentrating on his appeal. The last thing he needed was a distraction and trying to keep out of everyone's way was proving to be difficult. Delroy, Marcel and Jamal had entered the prison around the time Tommy was on remand and since he had been away they had bonded together and had been working their way up the prison ladder. Tommy had encountered them several times since his return and they appeared to have taken umbrage with the admiration Tommy had been receiving.

Tommy was busy reading the court documents and transcripts for his appeal when he heard the noise of saliva being sucked through teeth, a constant mannerism of Delroy. Tommy glanced up from his paperwork to see the three faces of Delroy, Marcel and Jamal peering around his cell door. Delroy gave a tilt of the head to Tommy's cellmate and he quickly slithered out of the doorway. Delroy stood in the middle of the cell and looked down at Tommy while Marcel and Jamal came in from the doorway to stand close behind Delroy.

"What are you reading boy?"

"A transcript from one of the witnesses for my trial"

"Ain't you got a lawyer to do that?"

"Yeah, I'm just making sure he's not missed something."

"You're the big man that killed a copper ain't ya?"

"I never killed anybody."

"So why you in here"

"I was set up."

"He was set up lads" He turned to the others and smirked. "Do you know what" Delroy whispered "I was set up to, what about you Jamal, why you in here?"

"I was set up weren't I?" He sniffed.

"What about you Marcel?"

"Set up man"

"You see, we were all set up. So what I'm thinking is that you could maybe look over our transcripts and check that our lawyers didn't miss somefing."

"Okay," Tommy was nervous.

"You would do that for us" Delroy pulled the spit loudly through his teeth.

"Sure"

"You never know, maybe you can find somefing that will prove we are innocent"

Delroy turned to the others and laughed. It was a fake laugh that sounded more like a snort and Tommy knew he was in trouble. He had seen them intimidate most of the other prisoners and anyone that stood up to them received a severe beating. If there was something they wanted he wasn't going to stop them. Tommy thought about making a run for it but how they stood, the whole doorway was covered, and where was he going to run to?

"I like your trainer's boy."

Tommy looked down at them. His mother had sent them to him only weeks before and they still had the glistening sheen to them.

"Give me them."

Tommy's face dropped in defeat. He slipped them off his feet and kicked them towards him.

"I like them jeans" Commented Marcel.

Delroy kept his stare on Tommy and pulled the spit through his teeth "Well what you waiting on boy?"

"I'm not giving you my fucking jeans" The words came out before Tommy realised what he had said.

Delroy sucked hard through his teeth as Marcel and Jamal took a step closer to Tommy's bunk. Tommy looked up anxiously at the three intimidating figures as they stared back at him.

"I ain't gonna ask again. Give me those jeans boy."

Tommy stood up from the bunk and was only inches away from them. He undid the top button on his jeans.

"Hurry up boy. I ain't got all day" Demanded Delroy.

Tommy undid the rest of the buttons on the jeans and started to slowly pull them down. Taking his jeans would mean having to wear prison trousers which were too big and baggy. With this train of thought, Tommy was now picturing the prison slippers, if he asked his mother to send another pair of trainers she would start to worry. Tommy felt a dull pain to the side of his head that stunned him back onto the bed. More blows hit him in the face and body. He tried to turn and fight back but his arms and face were pinned onto the bed. Then he felt his jeans being pulled off at the ankles.

'All this for a pair of jeans' He thought.

His underpants were then ripped from his body and his legs were kicked apart.

"Get fucking off me"

His shouting was muffled by his face being pushed deep into the mattress. He struggled as hard as he could but each time he pushed back he felt a hard blow to the side of his ribs. He heard the noise of the zip and couldn't believe what was about to happen. There was a low sound of Delroy sucking the spit through his teeth then Tommy felt something hard against his anus. He tried to clench together but his legs were held too far apart. He screamed like a wounded animal when Delroy's penis penetrated him. His heart was pulsing and he was in disbelief at what was happening to him. Each time Delroy pulled out, he would suck the spit louder through his teeth before thrusting forward once again. Tommy was hoping the screws would hear his cries and burst into the cell to stop it. The noise of the spit-sucking suddenly stopped as Delroy's breathing became faster. Tommy felt Delroy thrust several more times before moving away. Marcel released Tommy's arm and stood up from the bed.

'It was over' Tommy thought and tried to crawl further up the bed.

"Where do you think you're going?" Delroy grabbed Tommy's arm and jammed his leg between his own.

"Get off me you fucking beasts."

Tommy felt another hard blow in the ribs from Delroy and winced in pain.

"You like that huh?" Delroy whispered in his ear before punching him again.

"I'm gonna fucking kill you, I'm gonna fucking kill all of you" Tommy shouted.

Delroy laughed "You think so yeah" Delroy punched him in the back of the head twice and it made Tommy dizzy "Good luck with that you little faggot. When we're done with you today, we'll be back in here tomorrow and the next day and the next until your arsehole is begging us not to stop."

Marcel had his trousers down and spat on his hand before rubbing it over his penis.

"What the fuck are you doing?" Asked Jamal

"What, I ain't going in dry"

"Dry? He's just been lubed up from Del's Jizz, he's good to go, hurry the fuck up."

"Better to be safe than get a sore dick" Marcel smirked as he leaned forward and rubbed his penis up and down Tommy's anus.

"This ain't no pussy Marcel, get it in there" Jamal demanded.

Marcel aimed forward and rammed his penis into Tommy's anus. Tommy's muffled screams filled the cell.

Marcel was taking longer than Delroy and appeared to be in a rhythm, he stopped occasionally to shuffle forward as Tommy fought desperately to break free.

"Hold him still" Marcel groaned as his thrusts and breathing became shallower, he hardly had time to pull up his jeans before Jamal was ready to go.

"He ain't gonna feel that thing, maybe you should have gone first" Delroy commented on the size of Jamal's penis.

“Oh he is gonna fucking feel it alright” Jamal gritted his teeth and rammed his penis hard into Tommy’s anus.

“Help, somebody, help me” Shouted Tommy.

“Ain’t nobody gonna help you in here boy” Laughed Delroy.

Tommy was still clenching and fighting to break free whilst begging for someone to stop them.

“That’s it boy, keep fighting” The harder Tommy struggled the more Jamal appeared to enjoy it. In between thrusts Jamal clenched his fists and punched Tommy in the ribs “You like that boy”

Jamal made a face as his thrusting slowed and pulled back from Tommy.

“You can’t be done yet, boy. I think Tommy here was just getting into it” Said Delroy.

Jamal pulled up his jeans and as Delroy and Marcel released their grip on Tommy, he slid to the floor in a heap. Tommy looked up through his tears to see the three of them walk out of the cell. Delroy led the way, carrying Tommy’s trainers and Jamal at the rear with Tommy’s jeans slung over his shoulder.

Tommy’s cellmate returned and helped him up from the floor onto the bed. He had a painful burning sensation from his anus and could not straighten up due to the bruising on his ribs. His cellmate asked if he wanted to call the prison doctor but Tommy refused. He stayed curled up on his bed in the foetal position for most of the night.

In the morning, when Tommy stepped out of the cell to join the line for breakfast, some of the prisoners pointed and sniggered at the swelling on Tommy’s face, while others looked on in sympathy. They had heard every muffled scream and noise from Tommy’s cell but they did nothing. If they had uttered one word to the screws as to what was happening, they would be lucky to see out the day. His prison slippers were two sizes too big and the trousers were turned up several times to stop them from being caught under the heel of the slippers. Delroy appeared from his cell and commented on those close to him about his new trainers. He grinned when he caught sight of Tommy shuffling slowly further down the hall. Tommy knew the bruises would heal, but how was he going to live after the degrading act of being gang raped.

A couple of weeks went by and the bullying was becoming relentless. He was being nudged out of the way whenever they passed him and his food was being taken from his plate. With the prison issue clothing and his gaunt appearance, he was shuffling around the hall like an old man and no one would step forward to help. He cried silently in his cell each night and dark circles formed under his eyes through lack of sleep. He was on the verge of contemplating suicide, a common occurrence for young lifers and the only thoughts keeping him going was that if he was going to take his own life, he was going to take Delroy, Marcel and Jamal with him.

Chapter 18

Life in prison is a routine in itself but some prisoners have a routine inside their routine and the rapists were no different. They had a way of circling their prey and Tommy had been secretly circling them. From the second he rose in the morning, he was mentally preparing himself for what he was about to do. He was already a lifer and would be lucky to survive his sentence so it would make no difference how many more they piled on top. He picked up two spoons for his desert and held them tight together, it was something he had remembered seeing in an old prison movie years before. When he sat down at his table to eat, he managed to slip one into his pocket. Back in his cell, he began bending the spoon back and forth in the hope that it would soften the metal enough to break. After some time, he concluded that it was not working and so attempted to scrape the handle of the spoon along the wall in the hope of sharpening it to a point. Less than a minute later, he threw the spoon across his cell in despair. He wanted to scream out in anger. The tears started to flow down his face but apart from his heavy breathing, he did not make a noise. His inner turmoil was pushing him to breaking point.

He quickly grabbed the spoon back up from the floor and marched along the hall to Delroy's cell. He envisioned all three of them being there but when he entered the cell, and to Tommy's surprise, Delroy was on his own and had his back to him. Tommy grabbed him from behind and made repeated attempts to stab him in the throat with the spoon. It did not pierce the skin but the ferocity of the motion made him choke and struggle to breathe. He slipped from Tommy's grasp but could not shout for help due to his choking. Tommy dropped the spoon and pulled the sheet from the bed. He quickly pulled it around Delroy's neck and crossed his arms to tighten it. He attempted to fight Tommy off and they both fell to the floor with Delroy landing on top. Being much stronger than Tommy, he kicked and struggled for some time but it was all in vain as Tommy's only determination at that moment was to end Delroy's life. His arms and legs thrust a few more times before his whole body went limp.

Tommy knew Delroy was dead, but he held his tight grasp on the sheet for a while longer. The tears flowed down Tommy's face as the limp body of Delroy lay on top of him. He slowly pushed him to the side and stood up. When he looked down at the body on the cell floor he saw his trainers sticking out from under the bed. Tommy was planning to take his own life shortly, so had no use for them and left them as they were. He wiped the tears from his face with his sleeve and walked back to his cell, passing several other prisoners in the process.

A short time later, the prison alarm sounded, and the whole block was locked down. Tommy lay on his bed awaiting the screw's arrival to take him away to be charged with murder for a second time. He was expecting the screws to march in team handed with batons and face guards to drag him to solitary, a scenario that the screws appeared to take great pleasure in. It was several hours later that Tommy heard a light knock on the cell door and two screws entered.

"Tommy, I need you to come with me please."

Tommy never said a word. He stood up and was calmly led to the solitary block below. He stared at the bare walls and took a moment to take in his new surroundings before lying down on the metal bunk. For the first time in weeks, he felt safe. There was not the constant threat of Delroy, Marcel or Jamal bursting in to rape him again. He felt at peace as he curled up to enjoy the silence. That night in solitary was the first time since entering prison that Tommy had a proper night's sleep without being woken up by prisoners shouting or cell doors being slammed shut by the screws.

A couple of days went by and Tommy had still not been charged with Delroy's murder. He started to think that maybe he had not actually killed him and only rendered him unconscious. He wouldn't be charged with that as it would come down to Delroy having to make the complaint which even Tommy knew, would not be a good decision on Delroy's part. He was dreading being placed back on the hall and facing him again as he was sure that next time Delroy would kill him.

Tommy's cell door opened, and as before, two screws stood outside.

"Come with us Tommy, you're back on the block."

Tommy was scared. He didn't want to leave the cell.

"Come let's go, we haven't got all day."

Tommy shuffled forward and followed the screws back to the hall. When he reached the large steel bars of the gate to the hall he hesitated before continuing.

"Where am I going?"

"Same cell, off you go"

Tommy stepped inside the hall and watched the prisoners go about their routine. As he slowly walked along to his cell, he noticed that not one prisoner looked in his direction. Tommy was confused. When he entered his cell he saw his jeans and trainers laid out neatly on his bed. He picked up his trainers, and under closer inspection, he saw they were spotless. He picked up his jeans and brought them close to his face, they had a fresh smell as though they had been washed. Tommy threw off the prison trousers that he had been wearing and quickly put his jeans on. He was tying the laces of his trainers when a large dark figure filled his cell doorway. Tommy froze and had a fear that he was about to be attacked again.

"Someone would like a word," He said in a deep rough voice.

Tommy finished tying his laces and the large man tilted his head for Tommy to follow him. He had a rugged face and Tommy had seen him previously at the top table with several other men of a similar appearance. The man walked slowly and confidently along the hall landing, leading Tommy up a stairwell to one of the last cells on the top landing.

"Wait here," The large man said before turning into the cell doorway.

"He's here."

“Thanks, Butch, send him in” a hoarse voice came from the cell.

Tommy knew who it was from his time on remand. His name was Kingsley and he ran the prison. He controlled the drugs that came in, so, therefore, he controlled the prison. He had more control over the prisoners than the governor. The rugged man who Tommy now knew was called 'Butch' gave Tommy a tilt of the head for him to enter the cell. Tommy turned into the cell doorway to see Kingsley, an older man of average height with a hard expression.

“Tommy Ross. Have a seat” He gestured to the bed.

Tommy sat down nervously.

“I see you’ve got your belongings back.”

Tommy looked down at his trainers and back up at the older man.

“I thought I would return them to you after you left them in one of my associate’s cells, you know after his, shall we say, passing?” Kingsley gestured with his hands “The guy you took out worked for me.”

‘The guy I took out’ Tommy thought “So he is dead?”

“Oh, he’s dead” Kingsley smirked.

Tommy pondered.

“Look, I’m not condoning what he did to you. I know he was a nasty piece of shit and what happened to him had been coming for a long time, but to me, he was a good earner, I wouldn’t say he kept his mouth shut, but everyone has their faults, which, due to his faults, now leaves me with a problem…

“Why have I not been charged?” Tommy butted in.

The man put his fingers to his lips for Tommy to be quiet “I know some of the individuals in this place can be quite rude, their upbringing or whatever, but I thought most of you white boys had manners and knew not to interrupt when someone was talking.”

Tommy acknowledged his interruption and Kinglsey continued.

"As I was about to say, I now have a problem, I had something that needed to be taken care of, and your man Delroy was going to do this for me, but as he is no longer here, I now need someone else to take care of the problem"

"What kind of problem"

"I need someone taken care of"

"And you want me to do it?" Tommy asked, knowing the obvious answer.

"I think this might help your situation."

"My situation"

"Well you're situation, along with the answer to your question about not being charged I will now answer. You see, I used up a lot of favours to clean up what you did otherwise you would be sitting in solitary right now with another murder charge hanging around your neck. I know your next move is to go after those other two scumbags, so you have two options, you can take your chances and go after them without my backing, not a wise choice, or you can return this favour to me and I will not let anyone step in your way. I am of the understanding that you are going to be with us for quite a while, so if you do this favour for me, your time here will go very smoothly."

"You mean I will continue to be useful"

"Take it whichever way you like."

"Why don't you get one of your men to do it?" Tommy nodded towards Butch who was still standing by the cell door "I'm sure one of them would jump at the chance."

"Because Tommy, they are not owe me, if I get one of them to do it, that would mean I would then owe them. And anyway, as big as these guys are, they could never do what I'm asking you to do."

"What are you asking me to do?"

“I told you, I need someone taken care of.”

“You mean killed?”

“I never said that, but if I did, am talking to the right person? I mean, you are in here on a murder charge.”

“But I didn’t…”

The man gestured with his hand and Tommy didn’t finish his sentence.

“Also, I need you to understand, I will not help you in your quest for revenge, but if you do me this favour, I will make sure no one steps in your way”

“Can I ask what this person has done that he needs taken care of?”

“He hasn’t done anything yet. There is a trial coming up and he is going to give evidence in return for a reduced sentence. I’ve been asked to make sure that doesn’t happen.”

“Who is he?”

Kingsley smiled “I think it’s time for you to leave.”

Tommy walked back to his cell and lay on his bed. He pictured Delroy’s lifeless body on the cell floor.

‘I’m no killer, I’m no killer’ He said over and over in his head.

Chapter 19

As far as the authorities were aware, Delroy had committed suicide, but it did not take long for everyone in prison to know what really happened. Jamal had stepped up to Delroy's position and with a few new faces' recruited to his company, Marcel drifted into the background. Word had also spread that Tommy and Kingsley had spoken, but when no orders had been placed by any of Kingsley's men about Tommy, Jamal continued his reign of torment and Tommy watched his every move. His routine was slightly different from when Delroy was still around and he also had the new faces following him everywhere. He was still bullying and intimidating Tommy daily, taking food from his tray or slapping him in the head whenever he would pass him. Jamal was never on his own which was proving difficult if not impossible for Tommy to get to him. He had seen the occasional glances in his direction from Butch, waiting for an answer to give to Kingsley, but it wasn't until his path crossed once again with Jamal that Tommy gave them an answer.

Tommy stood in line with his tray for breakfast and was pushed hard out of the way. He knew it would be Jamal and turned to face him to show that he wasn't afraid of him.

"Look at this boy, I think he wants some" laughed Jamal.

Tommy stood firm and Jamal put his face closer to Tommy's.

"You wanna have a go? Come on, let's have it boy."

Tommy clocked the other two faces moving to either side of him. He knew he had no chance, he would be lucky to get a punch in on Jamal before they laid into him. The only good thing that would come out of this for Tommy would be the alone time he would spend in solitary. Tommy backed down and as Jamal passed him he turned back to face Tommy.

"I'll be back for those trainers boy" He looked Tommy up and down "And them jeans" He laughed before moving forward with his crew in tow.

Tommy knew what he had to do, he was not taking his own life without taking theirs first. He would rather die than suffer a life term of this every day. He saw Kingsley sitting at the top table surrounded by his men. Tommy made a point of walking by the table but Kingsley did not look up, Tommy locked eyes with Butch and discreetly gave him a nod. The message would be passed to his boss.

Tommy did not know his intended target and would have to wait it out until one of Kingsley's men made contact. He kept his head down and tried to stay out of Jamal's way. Marcel was still part of his crew but appeared to be further down the pecking order now that he had the new faces by his side. Soon after Tommy's nod to Butch, nobody appeared to bother him and now felt as though the other prisoners were moving out of his way when he passed them.

A few more days passed and Tommy had received notice that his parents were coming for a visit. He had not seen them for two months and he knew they would be keen to find out how their son was getting on. Since their last visit, Tommy had moved from the Feltham Young Offenders unit to Brixton prison and they were about to travel over 350 miles for a one-hour visit with their son.

Rashid, a prisoner who had been in solitary since before Tommy arrived, was recently released into the main hall. He had been sent there after a violent attack on another prisoner and made his presence known immediately. He was another bully boy and even the sight of him gave Tommy the fear. Before Tommy arrived in Brixton there had been a power struggle between Rashid and Delroy. With Delroy now out of the way, it was imminent that Rashid was going to take out Jamal.

Tommy's cell door was opened early before breakfast one morning and the large frame of Butch filled the doorway. He nodded to Tommy's cellmate who managed to squeeze out between Butch and the cell door frame. Once he was out of earshot, Butch handed Tommy a full bag of sugar along with the news that he had been dreading, Rashid was his target. It was an instant reminder of the time not so long ago when he was handed a similar bag of sugar to sabotage the Timex scabs cars.

"Rashid has a visit lined up tomorrow, he can't make that visit. He knows he is a target but you'll be the last person he suspects. Don't worry, he'll never see you coming, there are too many brothers in here for him to worry about"

Rashid was an informant, and the visit he had lined up was to give evidence. The prison hierarchy had decided that he was not to be killed but to be a constant reminder for other prisoners of what happens to an informant. Tommy knew what he had to do. He had witnessed the boiling sugar water being used in his time as a young offender. They called it napalm.

"I have a visit later today."

"Well, then you had better make a decision."

"It's my parents. I've not seen them in over two months."

Butch shrugged "As I said, you have to make a decision, if this guy talks, there are going to be a lot of pissed-off people out there."

Tommy sat down on his bed with the bag of sugar in his hand.

"Fuck"

Tommy's visit was scheduled for late afternoon. He knew his parents had boarded the early train from Dundee and would arrive at King's Cross after lunchtime. They would check into their hotel and make their way on the bus to Brixton prison. Although Rashid's visit was scheduled for the next morning, it would have to be done today and Tommy's only opportunity to get to him would be straight after breakfast. Tommy watched him closely in the food hall, he waited until he was nearly finished with his food and snuck out minutes before him. He rushed up to his cell and boiled the kettle. He had already pre-boiled it and the sugar was close by. He pressed the button on the kettle, it only took a couple of minutes for the second boil and Tommy quickly lifted the lid and tipped in the bag of sugar. He walked out of his cell with the kettle behind his back. Rashid was on the next landing down and Tommy had thought of pouring it from the balcony but there was a chance he would miss. He had to do this right. He walked down the metal stairs and flicked open the lid of the kettle. Rashid had an acquaintance in tow and both were smiling as Tommy approached them with the kettle behind his back.

"Get out of my fucking way if you know what's good for you."

Tommy stood firm.

"Are you fucking deaf or are you waiting on some more black cock up your arse?" He turned to his acquaintance and smirked.

Tommy was taken aback by the remark. His fear of this man disappeared as quickly as the boiling kettle was launched towards him. Tommy stood for a split second as the steam from the hot sticky liquid rose out from Rashid's melting skin. Tommy stared at Rashid's acquaintance before he casually turned around and walked back to his cell. He lay on his bed and waited. The alarm sounded and everyone was ushered to their cells and locked down. Tommy listened intently to the commotion in the hall. He heard the heavy footsteps of the screws approaching his cell door and as there was only one witness to the assault, he knew exactly who had pointed them in his direction. His cell door opened and the screws filed in behind each other in full riot gear. There would be no calm walk to solitary this time.

"Let's go Tommy" The first one shouted.

Tommy stood up and put his hands behind his back, he wasn't going to put up a fight with or without the riot gear but the screws still made a point of administering their punishment. The blows from their sticks knocked him to the floor and after a heavy hit to the head, he was knocked unconscious.

Tommy woke up in solitary, and with no sense of time, he did not know how long he had been there. His head and body stung with pain but it was nothing compared to missing out on his visit. Even if he was not placed in solitary he would have still missed his visit as the hall would have been locked down anyway due to the attack. His parents would have been turned away after travelling all that way to see him. He knew they would be more worried than disappointed and he would write to them as soon as he got the chance. Before long he would be dragged in front of the governor to have a few more months added to his twenty years. It was a bittersweet moment to be back in solitary and as he lay on the floor of the cell, he took in the comforting silence that was fast becoming his domain.

Chapter 20

A few things had changed in the hall since Tommy's month in solitary. The witness to the sugar incident had been transferred to the hospital wing after a beating, courtesy of Kingsley. Marcel had fallen out with Jamal and had been seeking out other prisoners to start up his rival gang. Tommy also noticed that nobody appeared to bother him anymore and other prisoners were giving him a wide berth. He had also received extra helpings of food and even some of the screws were nicer to him. With no one watching Marcel's back, he decided he would be the easier option until he could work out how to get to Jamal. With the word being put out from Kingsley not to go near Tommy he noticed that while he was watching Marcel, some of the other prisoners were watching him. Tommy heard a low knock on his cell door but when he looked up no one was in the doorway. He stood up and walked to the cell door and when he peered out another prisoner was several feet away.

"What do you want?"

The prisoner did not say a word and looked in the general direction of Marcel's cell before turning his back to Tommy. Tommy didn't understand until he glanced up and saw Kingsley and Butch on the walkway above. When they saw Tommy look up, they both looked towards Marcel's cell and turned their back. It was a signal. Tommy marched towards Marcel's cell. Unexpectedly, Marcel was waiting. A few punches were thrown between them until it ended up in a wrestle. Marcel was stronger than Tommy and managed to place him in a hold on the floor. He was continually apologising for what he had done which made Tommy angrier. He wriggled until his head was close to Marcel's face and sunk his teeth into his nose. The scream from a man in prison was rare and one of the last few times it was heard by the prisoners in the hall was from Tommy being raped, no one came then and no one was coming now. The noise echoed around the prison, through every cell, where every prisoner and guard could hear it, Tommy let the guy fall to his knees clutching his face, he could have walked away and left it at that but Tommy was so full of rage, he leaned towards the bed and pushed the mattress over a few inches, he grabbed Marcel by the back of his hair and with a full force, smashed his face into the metal bed frame. Tommy pulled Marcel's head back as the blood and teeth spitted from his mouth. Tommy released his hand from Marcel's hair and stood up. As he walked out of the cell he turned back at what he had done to see Marcel in a heap on the floor.

When Tommy got back to his cell he was still breathing heavily and his throat was dry. He licked around his mouth to gather some saliva and his tongue tingled with a metallic-like flavour from the sprays of blood. After a drink of water, his breathing gradually returned to normal. He put on a clean T-shirt and looked for somewhere to hide the bloodstained one. He thought about flushing it down the toilet but it would take forever to cut it into tiny pieces so that it did not get stuck. He threw it in a pile on the floor, lay down on his bed and waited.

Due to Marcel's injuries, an investigation was launched and once he was able to talk, he named Tommy as his attacker. As Tommy was being led back to solitary once again, it confirmed to him that he should have left him in the same way as Delroy so that he couldn't talk.

Before Tommy's release from solitary, he was to undergo a psychiatric evaluation, which consisted of several questions to determine if he had psychotic or sociopathic traits. Before his trial, while he was on remand, he had also been visited many times by a psychiatrist and learned very quickly of their agenda to categorise him. He read up on all their notes and remembered all the questions and knew what they are trying to do. Once he was categorised, they could use this to explain his behaviour and any actions he did in the future. He did not make it easy and refused to cooperate. With the governor informing him that more time had been added to his sentence, his chances of appealing and fighting his sentence was long gone. When he was released this time from solitary he was now going to be under close watch by the screws and the governor, but Tommy didn't care, he was already planning his move on Jamal.

With Jamal now moving up the chain, he swaggered through the prison as though he was untouchable and now had ambitions of taking over from Kingsley to bring in his supply of drugs from the outside. Kingsley knew Jamal was no threat and could have easily had him taken care of, but why would he owe that person when Tommy was going to do it for free. All he had to do was keep his word by giving the order to not stand in his way.

While Jamal was at breakfast, Tommy cunningly headed to the toilet. He entered one of the cubicles but did not lock the door. He was not sure which one Jamal would enter but if it happened to be the one Tommy was in, it would still work. He waited patiently and tried to control his breathing so that it was shallow. Tommy glanced down at the broken toothbrush, the sharp end barely sticking out from his clenched fist. As his mind raced back to Jamal raping him, he never once questioned what he was about to do.

He heard voices by the door of the toilet but neither of them was Jamal, it was his sidekicks.

"Wait at the door for me, don't let anyone in" It was Jamal's voice.

Tommy heard the footsteps and he began to shiver as though he was in a bath of ice. One of the other cubicle doors creaked and Tommy knew this was his only chance. He crept out from behind the door and glanced along to see the third door from the entry about to close. He marched forward and kicked it hard forcing Jamal back towards the cistern. Tommy reached up and ruthlessly forced the broken toothbrush downwards into Jamal's neck. Before Jamal had time to react, Tommy had slapped the end hard with the palm of his hand and cruelly watched the end of the toothbrush disappear. Jamal stumbled back further onto the cistern. Tommy did not wait around and walked fast towards the exit where the two sidekicks were waiting.

"Excuse me," Tommy said politely as he slipped between them.

They both stared at each other and rushed back into the toilet. The alarm sounded before Tommy made it back to his cell.

Everyone knew who had taken out Jamal, even the screws and the governor knew but not one prisoner talked. Tommy's reputation was now set, it was not what he wanted and he did not like the attention that it brought. He was now respected and also feared by the other prisoners. Not only did he have a reputation as someone not to be fucked with, but he also has the backing of the prison hierarchy. Some prisoners who had never given him the time of day were now asking if he needed anything, but this was not out of respect, it was out of fear. Tommy didn't trust them, and even though he was now protected, he knew they could turn on him without a second thought.

Other prisoners were now coming to him with propositions to take people out for a minor debt, but Tommy point blank refused. He wanted to be left alone and after a while, that's how things were, he had his routine of prison life, he read and studied and kept to himself. But to keep his easy life inside, now and then, Tommy would receive a nod from Kingsley and he had to take care of someone. These prisoners were not the run-of-the-mill junkies with a debt owed, they were rapists and child killers and to Tommy, they were fair game.

Chapter 21

Tommy was an early riser and enjoyed walking in the crisp clean morning air. He found comfort in the empty streets when there was little to no traffic on the road. He had also become acquainted with the faces that he passed by and was familiar with some of their morning routines of either waiting to be picked up for work, rushing to catch the early bus, or walking their dog. He would sometimes receive a nod or a faint smile in his direction and now and again there would be a passing comment about the weather, Tommy would reply courteously.

There was one dog walker that always made an effort to talk. He was a large man with a bad limp and Tommy always made a point to pause for a quick chat. As much as Tommy had observed these strangers' routines, talking to this man had now become a part of his. He had even started to carry some broken biscuits rolled in a tissue to feed the man's dog whenever he saw him, and seeing the dog run towards him wagging its tail gave him a happy, wanted, feeling.

"I think your dog likes me."

"I think he likes the biscuits more."

Tommy would've liked his own dog but living on Liam's fold-out sofa in his cramped flat wouldn't be an ideal situation. He knows Liam wouldn't mind but the living situation would have to change soon.

Tommy walked alongside the man and his dog and as they passed under a street light, Tommy noticed that he had a bruise around his eye and a few scratches on his face.

"Have you been in the wars?" Tommy pointed towards the scratches.

"Oh that, yeah I was jumped by some kids the other night," The man said, sounding a little embarrassed.

“That’s not good.”

“I usually time it so that I go to the shops when they are either at school or work, well that’s if any of them actually work nowadays.”

“When you say kids, you mean teenagers?”

“Yeah, they are between fourteen to maybe eighteen. I only nipped in for a couple of things and when I came out they were there. As I walked by they mouthed off and then I was hit over the back of the head. The next thing I know I was on the ground and the whole group of them were kicking the shit out of me.”

“Is it the same crowd that hangs around there all the time?”

“Yeah, it’s always the same faces. I normally go around the time when they’re not around, this is partly the reason I get up so early to walk my dog, I can’t risk taking him out at certain times in case I bump into them. I thought the older ones would be at work but I’m guessing if they hang around the shops at that time of day they don’t work.”

“Yeah it’s grim nowadays, I don’t think anything’s changed since I was that age. I remember being desperate for work and spending my days looking for a job, I never really got that thing of ‘let’s hang around the shops’”

“What is it you do Tommy?"

"I work with my son in his mobile car valeting business. I am looking for something else but unfortunately, I don’t have a trade, so my job options are kind of limited"

Tommy was careful not to mention that the qualifications he had gained over the years were done in prison. He wasn't embarrassed about being in prison but it was not a topic he cared to divulge to strangers. He also found it ironic that he only took the Timex job all those years ago because he had no qualifications and couldn’t get into a trade or an apprenticeship and now that he has qualifications he still can’t get a job due to his criminal record. Many years ago he might have been able to hide his criminal background in certain employment but due to disclosures, this was not possible. With his experience of court procedures through his many appeals and his years of studying law, he had thought about possibly setting up some sort of advice centre for helping wrongly convicted prisoners but that would only work if he had actually managed to overturn his conviction. This would also have to be a free service and Tommy needed a paying job.

As Tommy neared the edge of the park he saw the sun breaking through the clouds in the distance and made his excuses to leave the conversation. Picturing the teenagers beating up on his new friend made him a little angry but he put it out of his mind for the time being and made a mental note that he would enquire about them later, for now, his thoughts were on his own situation, he had been offered a bedsit flat, which was living, sleeping and cooking in one room with a separate bathroom. Liam had come to view the place with him and his first words were 'It's fucking tiny, you can't live here Dad' until Tommy pointed out that this was a like a palace compared to his living arrangements for the last twenty-two years. Tommy knew it didn't matter what kind of place they viewed for him to live, Liam would only see the bad points as he did not want Tommy to leave his flat. He liked having his father live with him but Tommy needed his own space. The job situation would have to stay for the time being as he needed to keep an eye on Liam and what was going on with his business.

Tommy marched along his usual route with the view almost clear in front of him, the buildings and hills were low and the sun was poking through the sky in the distance. He slowed his pace to take in the scene. It wouldn't last long as within the hour the same streets would be heaving with traffic with everyone rushing about their daily lives.

Tommy returned to Liam's flat and he was already up and out of bed eating his cereal.

"Close your mouth, Liam." Tommy stared at him. They both knew his Misophonia had kicked in.

"Sorry Dad" Liam closed his mouth and chewed his cereal more quietly.

Tommy picked up the appointment book with work scheduled for the day and scanned down the list of names. He cringed when he realised that three out of six of them were drug dealers and that Liam was going to be either picking up cash from them or leaving them a small packet in a secret compartment in their vehicle. Liam was a grown man and could make his own decisions but Ginge had an influence over people and Tommy thought he would have guided him away from this kind of thing, not make him a pawn in his business.

On their way to the first job, they were caught up in traffic lights and Liam picked up his bottle of water, he squeezed it gently making a crackling sound, he took a sip before letting it crackle back into its original shape. He continued driving and picked up the bottle three more times to take a tiny sip and crunched the bottle repeatedly. Tommy leaned over and grabbed the bottle from his hand and threw it out of the window.

"For fuck sake Dad"

"If you're going to take a drink, take a fucking drink, don't take a sip and then squeeze it again for another sip seconds later, take the fucking lid off it if you need to."

"It's designed to squeeze for a sip."

Liam concentrated on the road while Tommy stared out of the window. At another set of traffic lights, a man with a dog crossed in front of the work van and it reminded Tommy of his friend from his morning walk. He wanted to ask Liam about it but after the bottle incident, there was a slight animosity between them.

"I need you to do me a favour Liam."

"What?" Liam voice still had an angry tone.

"Ah it's nothing, forget it."

"No what is it?" Liam's tone lightened.

"There's a guy I talk to in the morning when I am out walking, he lives over the parkway, near the far end, and he was telling me he can't leave his house because of a group of lads. They jumped him when he came out of the shops. Can you find out who they are? Maybe tell them to lay off him."

"I can do that but only if you do something for me?"

"What?"

"Apologise for throwing my bottle out the window."

"Look, you know these noises fucking irritate me."

"Is that what you call an apology?"

"Look I'm sorry I threw your bottle out of the window. I'll buy you another one when we stop."

"No need" Liam smiled and pulled out another bottle from the side of his door and squeezed it to take a sip."

"You prick"

Tommy smiled and Liam pointed the bottle towards Tommy and pretended to squeeze the water on him.

"Can I ask you something, Dad?"

"That depends on what it is."

"What is the crack with this Misophonia?"

Over the years, Tommy had spoken to the prison Doctors about his condition and they hinted that it may be linked to something traumatic in his life that he has suppressed and has never dealt with. This immediately made him think of the rape but he was never going to bring that up. He had his take on how the Misophonia came about and he was sticking with it.

"It's a condition I picked up in prison. I think it's due to living in close company for so long. There's no cure, no medication, and the only solution I have found is to remove myself from the situation where there is a noise that is bothering me. This of course was extremely difficult when I was locked in a cell with someone for nearly twenty-three hours a day. If I can't escape from the noise, the irritation will turn to anger and I will become verbally aggressive to the person making the noise. In prison, if my cellmate was stirring his cup of tea too long, I would take it personally and start thinking of ways to hurt him. Once it starts I can't concentrate on anything but the noise. It then becomes like a fight or flight kind of thing. I have good days and bad days but it seems to flare up more when I am stressed or tired."

"Are you stressed now? I'm only wondering why it flared up about the bottle"

"No, it may just be due to my friend being beaten up" Tommy lied.

Tommy was stressed because he knew what Liam had been doing for Ginge. Although Liam was his son, he was also an adult and after being locked up for most of his life, he didn't really feel it was his place to say anything, but he did Ginge a big favour in prison all those years ago and only asked for one small favour in return, to look out for his boy, not have him selling coke. If Ginge saw that he was into that he could have guided him away from it, not make him a fucking dealer. All the youngsters were into drugs when they are out and about and it appeared to be a way of life for most of them, so Tommy guessed that Liam was no different, he was a popular lad and Ginge was using this as a gateway to supply them.

In the short time Tommy had been working for Liam, he had figured out almost every person that was dealing with Liam, even where they worked and lived. He also knew that when Liam picked up extra cash for minor jobs, it was a drug debt being paid, and if he could figure it out, it wouldn't be too hard for the police to figure it out either. It was now time to distance himself from his son, for his and his son's protection, because if Liam went down for dealing, Tommy would go down with him. He was out on license, which meant he would be hauled straight back to prison whether he was involved or not. If anyone was keeping tabs on Tommy, they would easily figure out what Liam was up to and he would be caught, if they were onto Ginge, they would soon enough be onto Liam and thus, repercussions for Tommy. It was a vicious circle.

Chapter 22

Liam was already outside waiting when Tommy appeared from the block to his new bedsit.

"I'm not late am I?" Tommy looked at the clock on the dashboard.

"No, I came early to sort out our schedule for the day" Liam tapped his pen on his appointment book.

"Is there a lot on?"

"Yeah, the work is kind of scattered, if there are no cancellations then we have a fair bit to get through, I'm just trying to work out which order to do them in so that we don't have to double back on ourselves."

Liam looked away as though he was in deep thought and tapped his pen some more on the book"

He wrote a couple of notes before tapping a few more times. Tommy tried his best to ignore it.

"How is the new pad? Are you settling in okay?"

Tommy was about to answer but clocked Liam's black eye "What the fuck happened to you?"

"Oh I eh, had a bit of trouble last night."

"What kind of trouble?"

"Ginge's brother Ritchie was at my door wanting money. I told him to fuck off and we had a bit of a scuffle."

"I'm only out of the house for two days and this happens."

"It's cool. Ginge said he was going to sort it out."

“Oh did he? And this is his way of looking out for you” Tommy mumbled.

Liam looked back to his appointment book and tapped his pen once again.

“Are you done?” Tommy nodded towards the pen.

“Eh yeah,” Liam could tell by his father's tone that he was annoyed but wasn't sure if it was from the pen tapping or his visit from Ritchie.

Liam started the van and drove off while Tommy stared out of the side window in silence as both the pen tapping and Ritchie’s visit to Liam made him think of his old cellmate Nate.

After another long stint in solitary for a violent attack, Tommy's sentence had now been extended to twenty-two years with parole. He had concluded that he was probably never going to be released and that he was slowly but surely becoming institutionalised. While some prisoners felt the immediate loneliness of solitary confinement, Tommy was overcome by how sheltered he felt from the petty prison goings on. He relished the solitude of solitary but couldn't work out if it was keeping him sane or driving him insane. While other prisoners merely existed until their release before they were back again for another crime, Tommy believed he was never going to receive that opportunity.

Once Tommy was back in the hall, he quickly adapted to his environment once again, and well aware that any one of the prisoners could take a dislike to him at any second. He had to watch his back constantly and studied their behaviour, their expressions, and their mannerisms. Some of them were lifers, blatant psychopaths who had no qualms about killing someone for little or no reason, and although he now had a reputation, he never got caught up in titles or labels. He would pick up a book and pretend to read when certain individuals were around so that they left him alone, but all the while he was carefully watching his surroundings. There was always someone new in prison who took Tommy’s quietness for fear but they soon paid the price. Whether it was a passing comment or a bullying nudge, Tommy stayed quiet but would always take revenge on anyone intruding into his personal space. He had become as ruthless and sadistic as any mindless thug that he had encountered, but only when he needed to be.

When Tommy was returned to his cell one day, he was welcomed by an older man who introduced himself as Nate. He had seen him in the yard several times but their paths had not crossed enough to make any sort of conversation. He took Nate to be a quiet reserved man who wanted to get on with his time in prison without any sort of drama. He was like a poster boy for the 'model' prisoner and this suited Tommy.

"Is that short for Nathan?"

"No, it's just Nate."

"Nate" Tommy confirmed, "That's cool."

"I noticed you end up in solitary a lot."

"Yeah, I don't mind it much. I enjoy the peace."

"I thought going there added time to your sentence."

"Sometimes, it depends on what they put me there for. Sometimes they hear something is about to happen so they put me in there until they can move a certain inmate, and sometimes they put me there just to cool off."

"So how much time has been added to your sentence since you've been in here?"

"I'm not sure, a couple of years."

"Wow."

"Don't you want to get out?"

"Sure. But I need to survive in here first."

Nate smiled "I can't argue with that."

"So what are you in for?" Tommy's first impression of Nate was that he was a good guy and he was hoping the answer to his question wasn't going to lead him to another bout in solitary.

"Murder"

"Yeah" Tommy had come across many murderers in his time in prison and he never took Nate to be one of them. "Same. But I didn't do it."

"Same."

Tommy smiled "No, I mean, I really didn't do it."

"Same" Nate smiled back.

"I noticed you hardly get many visitors. Do you have anyone outside of prison, wife, girlfriend, parents?"

"I had a few friends that used to make regular journeys down to visit but over the years that became less and less. Both my parents live up in Scotland so it's kind of hard for them to travel here as often as I would like. I also have a son."

"Wow, how old is he?"

"He'll be nine on his next birthday."

"No way, you have an eight-year son. You look far too young to have a son that age."

"What's he like?"

"I don't know. I haven't seen him since he was six months old. I receive photographs every once in a while from my parents and they let me know how he's getting on in school and stuff."

"Can't they bring him to see you?"

"It's complicated. My ex-girlfriend won't allow it. If they did it without her knowing and she found out, she would stop them from seeing him as well. What about you, you got kids?"

"I have an eighteen-year-old son. He's the reason I'm in here."

"What do you mean?"

"My son's a bright kid, studies hard, and he's never been in trouble. He was being bullied by a gang around our way. He kept it from us for a while, but I noticed the change in him and he eventually told us about it. It was proper nasty shit, beating him up, taking his books and ripping them up, they even set them on fire one time. There was one kid in particular who was always on his case, and one night, he followed him home. He was doing his usual, trying to goad him by slapping him in the head, spitting and kicking him. My son snapped, he'd had enough and turned to square up to him. This kid, who had been bullying my son relentlessly, and who towered over my son by several inches, stupidly pulled a knife. I think it was just to scare him, maybe he wouldn't have used it I don't know, anyway, shit happened, and my son managed to get the knife and stab him with it. He died right there on the spot."

"So what did you do?"

"I did what any father would do. I sent him to his room and told the police it was me. I couldn't have my son going to prison, he would never survive. If he did he would never be the same person when he got out."

"Could you not have pleaded self-defence?"

"Oh I did, they dropped it from murder to manslaughter, and even though we reported the ongoing bullying and also that it was his knife, they still gave me ten years. My family had to move away, they were under constant threat from the gang, they threatened to petrol bomb our home."

"I can imagine."

"Anyway, the way I see it, no matter what happens to me in here, no matter what I see or what I become, I have done right by my son and I know he is going to be okay. I have to fight mentally through some of the shittiest of days but I know that he's doing okay. This prison is like a revolving door to some people in here. They have nothing on the outside and have become institutionalised. If I can give you some advice Tommy, you need to break that habit of solitary. Try to have that one thing that's yours, that one place in your head that no one can take away from you and try to use it to get you through the dark times in here. If you don't have something to fight for, you're never going to get out."

"By the time I get out of here, my son will be older than I was when I came in here, he won't even know me. His mother will have filled his head with so much shit he won't even want to know me. He will never know that I was a good person and that I did try to do well by him but I kinda got caught up in shit. I'm in here for murder and he's going to believe I did it along with everyone else. Anyway, it doesn't matter, I've kind of accepted that I'm never getting out of here, I'm not exactly a model prisoner you know."

"Tommy you're letting them win. You're becoming what they want you to be. I see that you study the law" Nate nodded to Tommy's row of books. "That's good start, keep at it. You don't need to know everything, but enough so that you're one step ahead. Keep your guard up in here, keep it up high and watch your back but also focus on being free. Get rid of the negative thoughts and try to find your inner peace that no one or no environment can touch. Think of it as a test, don't let them win."

Nate had a soothing calm voice and Tommy found him pleasant to talk to, he wasn't like the other inmates who always appeared to be bragging or trying to prove themselves. Nate knew when to talk and could tell by someone's facial expression if they wanted to be left alone. Tommy enjoyed listening to Nate's advice. He had served three of his ten years and was now hopeful of winning his appeal against his sentence due to the evidence his incompetent lawyer failed to show at his trial. Tommy found Nate to be an intelligent man who would have made a great teacher or youth worker of some kind and thought his talents were being wasted in prison.

Tommy's only gripe with Nate was his eating habits. He was a loud messy eater. He tried hard to block the noises out but they would slowly creep up and push him to the point that they made him angry. Occasionally, Tommy would have a good day where he could block out the noise, but on a bad day, he would pick up other noises and one of them was Nate's sniffing. Tommy couldn't tell if Nate had always done it or if it was a new thing but to Tommy, it was like some sort of tick, and it reminded him of Delroy pulling the saliva through his teeth. Sometimes Tommy would walk out of the cell in mid-conversation with Nate to escape the noise.

The anxiety was mental torture and it affected Tommy's sleeping. He liked Nate but he was now having visions of hurting him. He had thoughts of hurting someone else so that he would be sent back to solitary to escape it. He knew of prisoners over the years that mentioned doors slamming or keys turning in the locks had made them go mad, but to Tommy, those noises were more soothing than Nates sniffing. During a moment of madness, Tommy sat up on his bed and screamed at Nate.

"Will you blow your fucking nose?"

Nate glanced over at Tommy who had his teeth gritted accompanied by a vicious stare "My apologies Tommy, I didn't realise I was sniffing" Nate said this more out of a reaction than an actual apology.

"Didn't realise, it's been going on for fucking weeks."

"Okay," Nate was taken aback by the change in Tommy.

"And you can stop tapping that fucking pen. Either write with it or fucking put it down."

"You seem very agitated Tommy, like very on edge. Is everything okay, is something else bothering you? Well, apart from the obvious of being locked up in this shit hole."

Tommy knew Nate was trying to brush over his outburst, he was a firm believer in that everybody had an off day, maybe even two, if a person has three off days in a row, that's an issue that needs addressing. Days later, Nate had been trying to control his sniffing habit but occasionally he did it without realising and Tommy's ears would perk up. If it happened a second or third time, Tommy would be riled up, by the fourth or fifth time. Tommy would be staring with the intent of attacking him. Nate asked the prison doctor for some antihistamines and although it stopped the sniffing, Tommy was now riled up at the way Nate slurped his cup of tea. If it wasn't the slurping, it was chewing with his mouth open. Tommy did have good days when nothing bothered him but Nate was starting to see a pattern. When Tommy was having a good day he enjoyed Nate's company, he would think over their conversations hours later and take mental notes of Nate's advice. It was around this time that Tommy began writing letters to Liam. He would send them to his mother and ask her to read them to him. He was hopeful that one day he would see him again but he was also prepared that if circumstances in prison turned bad, Liam would at least understand how much Tommy thought about him and wanted to be part of his life.

In prison, when one bully is transferred, released or taken care of by another prisoner, there is always another waiting in line to step up to take their place. Kingsley was the ultimate lifer and had everything set up where he controlled all the drugs coming in or out of the prison. No one could touch him, even the screws were paid extra to keep him protected, as long as no one interfered with his cash flow, he didn't care what went on around him. If someone came to him for help, there would have to be something in it for him or they would be due him a favour.

A new face had entered the prison by the name of Neville and after dropping the 'N' from his name he was more widely known as Eville, pronounced Evil. It did not take long for Eville to make himself known and one of his targets appeared to be Nate. Tommy had seen the eyeballing between them and brought it up to Nate.

"What's up with this guy, It's usually me they see as the soft target, why is he eyeballing you?"

Nate laughed it off "Maybe he needs a hug, I have longer arms"

When Tommy wasn't around, Eville was nudging Nate out of the way and whispering derogatory comments to him as he passed. Nate put on a front as though unfazed by all of it and never once mentioned it to Tommy. It was his problem not Tommy's and the last thing he would do was ask Tommy to sort out his problem. He could hardly give out advice to Tommy about staying out of trouble and keeping a clear head, and then in the same breath ask him to take care of some bully with a chip on his shoulder.

Tommy was having a bad day and Nate could tell by the way Tommy was fidgeting that something was bothering him.

"Tommy you okay?"

"I'm fine Nate."

"Come on Tommy, as much as my noises irritate you, your fidgeting makes me nervous."

"I'm fine" He snapped.

Tommy hated using the word fine. He could have used any word but in his context of moods, 'fine' seemed appropriate. He hated that Nate knew he was far from 'fine.'

He also hated Nate for slurping his cup of tea for the past twenty minutes. The hating had possibly started before that, maybe it was when he stirred it for longer than he should have, or maybe it was how slowly he poured it into the cup. Either way, Tommy's anxiety was extremely high and it was time to take a walk out of the cell before the visions of hurting him returned.

Tommy left the cell and took a slow walk around the hall. He gave the other inmates a nod as he passed. He had the respect of most people as they all knew what it meant to cross his path. As he walked passed the pool table he cringed when the cue smacked the white ball hard before it clunked into several other coloured balls. He had come out of the cell to escape Nate's noises and now other things were getting to him. He kept telling himself that it would pass and that he was only having a bad day. He glanced up and saw Kingsley leaning over the barrier of the gantry. Kingsley tilted his head in a gesture that he wanted to talk so Tommy made his way up the metal stairs to the top landing. Kinglsey stood by his cell door.

"I thought you would have come to me to stop it."

"Stop what?" Tommy was confused.

"The business with Nate"

"What business?"

"What business? You've just come out of your cell and given the nod."

"The nod for what"

"Tommy" Kingsley pointed down to Tommy's cell and they both looked stared over the metal rail to see Eville marching towards Tommy's cell where Nate was left on his own."

"Fuck" Tommy took the metal stairs and descended them two and three at a time.

"NATE, NATE" He shouted as he hurried across towards his cell"

It was too late, Eville brushed passed Tommy as he walked out of the cell and Tommy saw the spray of blood on his hand. Nate was lying on his side with a piece of metal sticking out of his lower back.

"NATE, NATE" He was still breathing but staring out in shock. Tommy shouted from the cell door "HELP."

One of the guards marched over and set off the alarm. The other screws came running and the hall was quickly placed into lockdown. Tommy was escorted to solitary for twenty-four hours before he was allowed to return to his cell. He had heard word from one of the screws that Nate was still alive but in a bad way. When he was returned to his cell he found it nearly empty, all of Nate's belongings had been removed and the blood had been cleaned up. It was a poor job as he could still see the stains from where the mop had been used to wipe up the blood. Tommy stepped back out of the cell and looked along the landing towards Eville's cell. His first port of call was Kingsley and as he ascended the metal stairs, Butch appeared from the cell next to Kingsley's. He raised a finger for Tommy to wait. After a short word with Kingsley, he gave Tommy the nod to enter.

"I know why you're here Tommy but I can't allow it. You gave him the nod."

"I was angry. I don't even remember who I gave the nod to."

"Whether you knew or not, you still gave the nod. If I let you go after him it will turn into a free for all."

"What was it about? Why did he target Nate?"

"You don't know?"

"I guess not."

"The guy that Nate killed was part of his crew"

"Nate knew it was coming. He never mentioned it to you."

"He never said a word," Tommy thought about mentioning that it was Nate's son that did the killing but he kept it to himself. Not that it would have gone any further than Kingsley's cell but he didn't feel the need to tell him. It was between him and Nate.

"I could've stopped it. I guess he didn't want you involved."

"Or want me owing you."

"Maybe" Kingsley shrugged.

Tommy remembered Nate's advice, about not letting them win. It was quiet when he returned to his cell and although there was some noise in the hall, it was nothing that bothered him. There was no slurping or lip smacking or any other weird noises to irritate him. He was going to miss Nate, it was a bittersweet moment. There would be a new cellmate soon enough but for now, he would enjoy the silence. He was going to use Nate's advice and concentrate on his release, but first, he had to see the prison doctor, it was time to find out about the noises that were making him angry, angry to the point of violence.

Chapter 23

"So why did you leave for London?"

Liam had been building up to asking his father the question all morning. He had possibly wanted to ask him since he had come out of prison. If he was truthful with himself, he had wanted to ask the question since his first visit to his father all those years ago. However long it was, he had said it, it wasn't the exact wording he wanted to use but the question was out there now, and the answer he was waiting on would hopefully explain why he had walked away from him at six months old.

Tommy turned his head towards his son and looked away a little embarrassed.

"Love" He mumbled.

"Love" Liam scoffed.

"Love" Tommy confirmed.

"I was always led to believe you left me because you had practically been brainwashed by the militants, that they had filled your head with so much hate and anger that you were a danger to be around" Liam managed to twist the question to Tommy not only leaving but leaving his son.

"Who told you that, your mother?"

"No, I kind of picked up bits and pieces from other people when I was growing up. They made out as though you were a dangerous man."

"Do I seem like the type of person who can be brainwashed?" Tommy couldn't believe Liam's perception of how things happened back then. He pondered on the dangerous man thing and yeah, he could be categorised as such now, but not back then.

"I was messed up, sure, but I didn't leave you to join the militants. I left because I was being pushed away, no matter what I did, your mother would turn it against me and stop me from seeing you. After we split up I still had all these feelings and passion to be with someone and it just so happened the only girl that gave me any attention was a militant that lived over four hundred and fifty miles away. She kept in touch and while I was being pushed to my limit by your mother, one day I said 'fuck it' I'm going to London."

"What do you mean she pushed you to your limit, what happened?"

"I had already been warned to stay away from your mother, no contact, that sort of thing, but from my point of view, I hadn't done anything wrong. It was your mother that had been sneaking around with Martin, she was the one that had done wrong, yet they were punishing me by not letting me see you. Anyway, one day I saw Martin pushing your pram, I thought your mother was close by so I held back, but as I trailed on behind, I realised he was on his own with you. As angry as I had been about the whole situation, something told me to rise above it, go over and talk to him and sort things out, maybe he could persuade your mother to make some sort of arrangement and see things from my side. I had nothing to lose so I shouted after him. When he turned and saw me he started walking fast to get away from me, so I ran to catch up.

'Martin, wait up' I said 'Look, I don't want any trouble. I want to try and sort things out.'

'Sort things out, as far as I am concerned that is in the court's hands' it felt like your mother's words, not his, not someone who had been my friend all those years. 'Look, I thought you would maybe try and mediate the situation and talk to Jade for me so that I can maybe see my son.'

'See your son' He stared at me 'He's my son now' He said smugly and brushed me off like a bit of dust on his jacket.

It was the lowest most despicable thing anyone could have said to me at that point in my life. The 'oh he's only trying to provoke me' thing was long gone after hearing that."

"What a fucking prick, so what did you do?"

"I don't remember hitting him, all I remember was being pulled off him and his head was lying back on the pavement with his face covered in blood. I shrugged off the people holding on to me, I grabbed the pram and wheeled you away. The police were called and when they turned up to my flat I was charged with kidnapping my own child. I somehow got bail and my solicitor informed me that If I contacted them again in any shape or form, I would be remanded until trial, also due to my actions it was now going to be a long hard fight for access. Your mother started to tell anybody and everybody that I was some sort of psychopath. I remember calling her soon after and she was screaming down the phone 'You're not allowed to call here,' I told her 'You were the one sneaking around sleeping with that slimy bastard behind my back so you can tell as many lies about me as you want but when my son grows up he's going to know the truth' She said 'No he won't grow up to know that because he won't even know who you are.' About an hour later the police were at my door and I was charged again with breaking a non-contact agreement. They didn't lock me up though, in hindsight, maybe they should have.

My solicitor contacted me with a condition from their solicitor that they would drop all the charges against me if I never contacted them again, sign you over to them to play happy families and give up any rights I had as a father. This was the second time they had offered this deal, only this time, I had several more charges against me. I was starting to see a pattern, they provoke me, I react, they get me charged, and then they put this offer to me. I think their plan all along was to get me out of the picture.

It was also around this time I received another call from Nile, she knew something was wrong. I had messed up, not only the fact that I wasn't getting to see you but also someone I once trusted was now playing dad to you. Anyway, she was always asking me to come to London to see her and the way things were, I knew I needed to get away from the situation, even for a few days to clear my head and work out my next move. I slept on it and the following day I had made up my mind that I was going.

I waited on your mother as she left your grandparent's house with you and I approached her, she did her usual mouthing off at me about not being allowed to talk to her, I never said a word to her, I put my hand up in a gesture for her to shut up. I looked into the pram and said 'You'll always be my son, no matter what and I will always fight for you. I walked away with tears in my eyes"

"I can't believe I have never heard any of this before."

"Well, now you know what drove me to London. It was only meant to be temporary."

"It was still kind of temporary"

"Yeah I suppose"

"Love eh?" Liam made a face at Tommy and they both smiled.

Tommy stepped off the train at Kings Cross station in London. He had called Nile on one of two temporary numbers that she had given him. The first one he tried there was no answer but the second number he took to be a call box as each time he called, it took a long time for someone to answer and it was mostly random people passing that picked up the receiver. He confirmed his train times and Nile said she would meet him at Kings Cross in time for his arrival. Tommy walked out of the station with his small rucksack containing enough spare clothes to last him a few days, but depending on how things went with Nile, he could stretch it out for a week.

He looked around for Nile but couldn't see her anywhere. As he stood taking in the busy scene in front of him he caught sight of someone staring and smiling. It wasn't until she started to wave that he realised it was Nile. She was not how he remembered her. Her hair was matted, her clothes looked dirty and he couldn't tell if her clothes were baggy or she had lost a lot of weight, either way, they were hanging off her. As she got closer she took a draw of her rolled-up cigarette, something he hadn't seen her do in the time he was with her.

On the train journey down, Tommy had visions of their reunion, both of them running into each other's arms like long-lost lovers or something, but it turned out to be a bit of an anti-climax. When she leaned in to kiss him her clothes smelled like she hadn't washed in a week. He couldn't believe how much she had changed in the short time they had been apart. Tommy kissed her back but was standoffish.

"Is everything okay? You seem different" Nile asked.

"I'm fine, it's been a long day" Tommy lied. He was not 'fine' He was ready to about-turn back into the station and board the first train home to Dundee.

Nile took his hand and led him towards the bus stop "Come on, everyone is in the pub, they can't wait to meet you."

Tommy caught her eye and felt warmth from her smile, it gave him a wanted feeling he hadn't felt since their first night together, and it was enough for him to put his despondency aside.

Nile and Tommy arrived at The Winchester, the latest pub she had been frequenting. There was always a pub close by to whatever house they were currently occupying, illegally of course.

From the outside, The Winchester had the presence of a middle-class pub due to the large up-market properties that surrounded it, but as Tommy followed Nile through the large wooden doors, he found the inside to be far from middle-class. The first thing that hit him was the smell, the same unwashed musty smell from Nile only much stronger. He looked around the pub and recognised Oliver, Stevie and Katie amongst some of the faces staring back at him, all friendly smiling faces. Callan, whom he had met briefly after his arrest in Dundee, was the first to approach him and welcome him into their company. Tommy's image of Callan after his brief meeting in Dundee hadn't changed, his long straggly hair, almost like a perm that was thinning out, his big fluffy coat with the collar up and even though he stunk like the rest of them, there was still a sort of coolness about him. He was very polite with a relaxed manner and he reminded Tommy of an old-school hippie from the sixties, or what the media stereotyped as a sixties hippy should be like. They both found a seat close to the bar and Callan placed a pint of beer in front of Tommy.

“The first one is free, you need to earn the next one” Callan winked.

Throughout the evening, Tommy listened to them chat and was gradually introduced to most of the group. Some of them had weird names or nicknames that they had possibly picked themselves and most likely thought were funny at the time but now that the names had stuck, they sounded stupid. Now and then Nile would squeeze Tommy’s hand and lean in to kiss him. He felt a little fuzzy, and it made his first impression of Niles's appearance and the constant smell from the group fade slightly, but Tommy suspected this was due to the alcohol. At closing time, Tommy picked up his bag and Nile linked her arm in to his as they followed the group out of the pub. Tommy didn’t have to walk far for his accommodation for the night. It was a three-floor townhouse, only a stone’s throw from the pub.

At one point the building was lived in by a rich family but over the years as each family member moved on and the older owner was taken into care, the home was left to deteriorate. The original features were untouched, including the fireplaces that were situated on each floor. This meant the new residents were able to heat the whole house by burning whatever rubbish they could find. There was running water but no electricity so it was a cold bath for washing which Tommy noticed not many of the group appeared to bother with.

“Come on, come on, follow me” Nile said as she ran up the stairs “I’ll show you my room.”

Tommy followed Nile slowly and was careful with his footing as the stairs were in darkness. She waited on the first landing and took his hand to hurry him up to the second level. They entered a large room and even though it was dark there was enough light coming in from the outside to see their way in the room. There was an old wooden bed with a sleeping bag and some spare covers were strewn across it. Tommy walked over to the bay window and glanced down to the street below, one of the side windows was cracked and the other, although in tack, was boarded up. He found this strange and thought the cracked window should be the one that was boarded up.

"In case you're wondering I cracked the window when I was removing the board so I thought I would leave the other one in case I broke that as well."

"How did you know I was thinking about that?"

"I'm psychic."

Nile lit a candle and Tommy saw her smile. He placed his bag on the floor and sat on the bed.

"What a lovely home you have here!"

"I've slept in worse places."

"I bet you have."

Tommy pictured Nile sleeping in some pissy shop doorway with cardboard boxes to keep her warm. Nile came closer to Tommy and put her arms around him. The few pints of beer had gone to his head a little but it did not disguise the smell from Niles's clothes. They started to kiss but were soon interrupted by the noise from others running up and down the stairs or banging and screaming in the room above them.

"Is it always like this?"

"Pretty much, they're just having fun."

"It sounds like a party without any music."

"Don't speak too soon."

"What do you mean?"

"You'll see."

Nile pulled Tommy back onto the bed and began kissing once again. Tommy heard the sound of a guitar and the tapping of feet on the floor. Moments later voices were singing along in time to the tune being played on the guitar. Tommy and Nile both laughed as they lay back on the bed in each other's arms listening to the song as more people joined in.

Tommy was woken by a mixture of creaking floorboards and voices in the surrounding rooms. He checked his watch, he had slept much later than he normally would, he wasn't sure if this was down to the alcohol or if it had been a long day of travelling, either way, he knew his body must have needed the extra few hours' sleep.

He could make out Nile and Callan's voice in the room next door, they were discussing details of a march and several times the name Stephen Lawrence was mentioned. Tommy was familiar with the name. He would have to have been hiding under a rock to not have heard his name as it had been all over the TV and filled every newspaper for the last six months. Stephen Lawrence was a black teenager who was murdered in a racially motivated attack while waiting for a bus. He was only eighteen years old, the same age as Tommy.

Tommy got up from the bed and put his clothes on. He could hear the voices of Callan and Nile getting louder, almost as if they were arguing, but when Tommy ventured through they glanced at him and continued their discussion in a quieter tone.

"What going on? What's all this?" Tommy looked up at the map taped to the wall which had marker lines drawn on it.

"We're discussing our route for our demo."

"Cool, what's it for or against should I say?"

"It's a demonstration to demand the closure of a bookshop that's being used as a headquarters for the BNP," said Nile.

"Nile wants us to march right up to the shop but the police have informed us that we won't be allowed, so we are trying to work out an alternative route."

"I think it's a waste of time. If we don't make a proper statement, what is the point of the march? I mean since when did we start doing what the police said."

"I think you have a proper radical on your hands there Tommy."

"That's fine by me."

Callan smiled at them both and while Tommy returned the gesture, Nile kept her serious almost frosty expression.

"Nile you know this is not even our demo, it's being coordinated with the Anti-Nazi League and the Youth Against Racism in Europe, and they asked us to join them so we are spectators. I can put it to them, but they are adamant they don't want any drama, after what happened to Stephen, they want a peaceful demo."

"A peaceful demo, do they have any idea what we are about?"

"Look, I'll make a call to set up a meeting and see what they want to do, but the impression I got from them was that they wanted to be loud and get noticed. We are basically there to make up the numbers" Callan dug in his pocket for some change "I'll go and make that call."

Nile followed Callan to the stairs.

"It's okay Nile, it's just a quick call. Stay here and check on the others, remind them about the banners, no swearing, no vulgarity and no reverse racism"

Nile hovered at the top of the stairs and when the front door slammed shut, she turned to Tommy and brushed passed him to go to her room.

"What's up? Is everything okay?" Tommy followed Nile to the window as she watched Callan go to the phone box across the street.

"Its fine, come on let's check on those banners."

Tommy ascended the stairs to follow Nile to the top level of the house. He couldn't help but notice the graffiti-covered walls. He hadn't noticed any of it last night as the stairs were in darkness. He couldn't believe someone would do that to a person's home, even if it was abandoned many years before. He didn't mind graffiti if it was artistic, he admired some of it, especially some of the spray paintings he had seen in films of New York subways, but what they had done in this house was not art, it was sheer vandalism, and someone at some point in the future was going to move into this house, maybe someone with young kids and the mess that they have left was disgraceful.

Tommy reached the top landing and both bedroom doors were open. In one there appeared to be several tins of paint scattered around and people hard at work making placards. Tommy peered around the door and the large sheet was laid out on the floor with stencilled letters that read 'NO TO BNP,' they were being painted in thick bright red.

"What do think of our workshop?" Nile asked.

"Like Santa's Elves."

"Grab a brush, we have quite a few more to go" commented Stevie.

"I'll need to use the toilet first."

"Yeah, good luck with that" He smirked.

Tommy was hesitant before opening the door of the toilet but as it creaked open it didn't appear too bad, there was certainly less graffiti. He opened the lid on the cistern and he got what Stevie meant. It was filled to the brim with shit. Tommy closed the lid and marched back out of the toilet. He curiously walked into the other bedroom and saw Nile by the window. He knew this was the bedroom above Niles as it also had a bay window. There were a couple of mattresses on the floor with empty tins of beer that had been used as ashtrays but the guitar leaning on the wall in the corner confirmed Tommy's thoughts. He walked over and stood behind Nile. He caught sight of Callan still in the phone box putting in more change to make another call.

"He's a busy man" Tommy commented.

"Oh my god, I never heard you come in."

"I just saw the toilet, I really couldn't go. I'm just going to piss outside."

"Oh yeah, no one uses that one, it's been blocked since we came here. There's a toilet on each landing" Nile said without turning from the window.

Tommy saw Callan hang up the receiver and walk in the opposite direction from the house "Is everything okay?"

“Yeah of course” Nile forced a smile but Tommy was not convinced “The toilet on the landing downstairs is the cleanest. Come on.”

Tommy followed Nile down the stairs and she turned and pointed to the door opposite her bedroom.

“Give them a hand with the painting, I won’t be long”

Nile rushed down the stairs and Tommy about turned from the toilet and headed into Nile's bedroom, he went straight to the bay window and saw Nile walk fast before breaking into a jog to cross the road in the direction that Callan had went.

Tommy didn’t like what was going on. His head was filled with questions. ‘Is there something going on between Nile and Callan? If there is, why did she persuade him to travel all the down here, to make him jealous?’ After everything Tommy had been through with Jade, he had no time for mind games. He wanted to grab his bag and leave but after visiting the toilet he somehow ended up back upstairs helping the others paint the banners.

Nile returned soon after, and Callan was not long behind her. Nothing was said to Tommy and hardly any of the others spoke to him, they hardly even spoke to each other unless it was something to do with the demo. There was hardly even a smile until Callan shouted ‘pub time’ and they immediately stopped what they were doing and started chatting like normal people. Even Nile changed from being almost robotic to having a few puffs on her rolled tobacco, and she was once again all over Tommy. On the way to the pub, Tommy pulled Nile aside.

“What the hell is going on? Am I missing something here?”

“What do you mean?”

“Why is everyone so serious, yet when Callan snaps his fingers it’s like a signal for everyone to enjoy themselves?”

“It’s not like that.”

"From what I've seen it is, I've been helping them paint for hours and nobody has even made an attempt to talk to me but as soon as Callan shouts 'pub time' they are all patting me on the back saying 'good job'"

"What can I say, Callan pays the wages and they have a job to do, maybe they don't want distracted."

"Pays the wages, from where? He's a fucking lobby dosser like the rest of them."

"Lobby dosser? Don't be fooled, Tommy. He brought us all together, a large group of people with the same beliefs to help the oppressed. He calls the shots, well actually I think someone else calls the shots but Callan is our frontman for the group. What's the matter, I thought you wanted to be part of this?"

"I do, it's just a very strange set-up, and it feels like a bloody cult."

"Hardly" Nile smiled "Tommy, you can leave whenever you want, but I really would like you to stay. I like you, you know that. I wouldn't have asked you to come all this way would I?"

Tommy shrugged and Nile moved in closer to him and placed her hands on his hips.

"Listen, the demo is coming up very soon and we'll have some fun okay? Now come on, let's get a drink."

Tommy felt his hand being pulled and he let Nile lead him towards the pub.

Chapter 24

Tommy got the impression that the landlord was not too pleased with his new crowd that was now frequenting his pub. He had taken on the lease of a pub in an up-market part of London and his clientele had virtually changed overnight, but what could he do, he knew they were trouble, he knew they were the type that were always looking for something to react to, something to be offended by. If he had asked them to leave they would have thrived on the attention and caused more bother than it was worth. He had to wait it out, they would move on eventually. In the meantime he would serve them with his fake smile, and bide his time until they were physically evicted from their dwelling to take up residence elsewhere.

Tommy liked their fight, their cause when it came to taking on authority, but he resented their attitude when it came to small local businesses trying to make a living. He got the impression that they would happily watch someone's livelihood suffer out of spite.

When Tommy woke up on his second morning in the house it was much like a repeat of his first day. The group were busy painting and making signs while Callan and Nile discussed the finer details of the march. Tommy could sense the tension in the group. They were on edge whenever the march was mentioned. It was confusing for Tommy, this was their thing, this was supposed to be what they were about, fighting for injustice, and they should have been excited, not nervous. Nile was constantly on Callan's case but he would never give her a straight answer and the more she leaned on him for answers the more blasé he became about it. He always had to 'make a call' as though he was asking someone for permission which seemed to antagonise Nile even more. When Tommy witnessed them in action at the Timex strike they were co-ordinated to the finest detail. They were well-organised and ready to take on the might of the authorities with no fear of repercussions from the police. What Tommy was seeing now was a group of people waiting to be told what to do by their leader. He could sense that Nile was seeing what he was seeing and maybe this was the reason she was giving him a hard time. She had sold their purpose to Tommy to bring him on board and she was perhaps embarrassed that she knew Tommy was now seeing it for what it was.

"Why are you so laid back about this march Callan?"

"Laid back?"

"Well, we've attended how many protests together?"

"I don't know, a lot" He smirked.

"I don't mean up and down the country, I mean in London alone, how many?"

Callan shrugged "I don't know. What's your point? Where are you going with this?"

"Well, there always seems to be a bloody protest in London, whether it is left versus right, rich versus poor or whatever, and we are always first in line, taking on anybody that's against the government, big business, police or whoever, but now we are up against black versus white you are taking a back step."

"Where is this coming from?"

"Well, you are a predominantly white male as most of the group are and it would be a massive attraction for the press if you were all pictured at the front of a large black majority crowd fighting against racism."

"Don't you think that will make us the main target for the police? As well you know, this march is not only about the BNP, it is about the police dragging their heels in an investigation of the murder of a black male by four white males."

"Since when did you worry about the fucking police?"

"Since I received a concussion at our last march from a crack over the head by a wooden stick they like to call a truncheon, and I know they'll be out in force to show their authority due to the criticism of their handling of the case"

"Not all of the police are racist Callan."

"Maybe not, but they are all hated by everybody, they are bullies, brainwashed bullies. I'll give you an example, if there was a protest against say the government's stance on fox hunting, and one of the officers policing the protest was an animal lover but he had strict instructions from his superiors to come down hard on those protestors. Would that officer step in or even question why his colleagues were dragging some poor defenceless old lady by the scruff of the neck out of sight of the press and cameras to smack her around with their wooden sticks? No, he'll shut his gob, turn away and say 'Just doing their job mam.' So, to answer your question, am I hesitant to lead the way in front of thousands of the black community, against the police who don't want us to walk past a certain bookshop that is the BNP headquarters, while chanting that the police are full of racist pigs, then yeah, I'm fucking hesitant" ranted Callan

Nile stayed quiet and so did the rest of the room until Callan followed up his little speech moments later with 'I know it's early but fuck it, let's go to the pub."

16th October 1993

The British National Party (BNP) is a far-right fascist political party and was founded in 1982 by former members of another fascist group the National Front. In 1989, they opened an office in a bookshop on Upper Wickham Lane in Wellington South London which serves as their headquarters. The same area began to have a large increase in racist attacks and four years later on the 22nd of April 1993 while waiting for a bus in Well Hall Road Eltham, Stephen Lawrence was murdered. The police investigating the murder were being accused of being corrupt and incompetent and some of the investigating officers were also racist after failing to follow leads or arrest suspects only days after the killing on reasonable suspicion alone, a basic point of criminal law. The family of Stephen Lawrence were also being smeared and discredited.

The day of the march came and as Tommy had imagined, the group's attitude had changed and appeared excited while they talked and laughed among themselves. The night before, a large van had pulled up outside the house and the group helped load it up with the banners and placards that they had been working on. Callan gave each of them a final check as they were being loaded up. The van would be parked close to the start of the march and each of them would be handed out amongst the crowd. Callan called a meeting once everyone was awake.

"Okay guys, I have received information that the police will be in full riot gear, they are saying they've had a tip-off from the BNP and are expecting trouble, but we all know how these things work. If we encounter any BNP groups along the way, do not react, that's what they want."

"Yeah that's if they are BNP members" Stevie said.

"What do you mean?" Tommy asked.

"Sometimes the police go undercover and pretend to be one of the protesters to start shit."

"Really"

"It happens all the time Tommy" Katie added.

"Ello, Ello, Ello, what's going on ere then? Peaceful demos, we can't av none of that, let's be avin ya. Come down ard on em, especially em bloody militants, nothin but trouble. Arrest em all, we need to justify our budget" Oliver imitates an officer.

A few of them snigger before Callan expresses "Guys, just be careful, I know we've done this a long time now and I'm all for a bit of action but this is a hot topic and the spotlight is on this march. The police are not getting dressed up in riot gear for nothing."

As the group are leaving the house to make their way to the start of the march Tommy pulled Nile aside "Are you okay, everyone seems excited but you look nervous."

"I'm fine, I'm just a little disappointed in Callan's pep talk, I mean, I kind of got the feeling he wants us to run for the fucking hills if we see a police officer."

"Yeah, it wasn't very inspiring."

"I am fine though Tommy"

Nile smiled and Tommy knew it was forced. He also hated the word fine, he had read somewhere that when a person used the word fine, it meant they were hiding how they truly felt, that it was more of a decision rather than a condition.

"Listen if you don't want to go today its cool. I mean I know I've come all this way and I'm here to support whatever the cause you guys are fighting for, but I'm only here to be with you Nile."

"That's sweet Tommy but really I'm..."

"...Fine" Tommy finished her sentence.

"Come on. Let's catch up with the others" Nile pulled on Tommy's hand.

The march was to start on Winn's Common in Plumstead and as they drew closer more and more people joined them. They were still a mile from the Common and the group had stretched to several hundred. Nile grasped Tommy's hand tightly and gave him a wide smile as they both took in the faces surrounding them. Although it was never mentioned between them, he now classed Nile as his girlfriend. He had travelled a long way to be with her, she had slept in his arms each night since he arrived, so he was sure it was enough to class her as his girlfriend. He felt proud, a skinny white boy from Dundee walking hand in hand with his mixed-race girlfriend, surrounded by mostly black people to support them against the racist BNP.

As the crowd become tighter, Tommy received many nods from strangers. They were acknowledging his support and appreciated him for being a minority in the crowd. Callan had mentioned several times that they were going to stand out in the crowd, but with Nile by his side, he didn't mind.

They turned the last corner to Winn's Common and Tommy couldn't believe what he was seeing. It was a sea of people, he had no way of knowing how many but he could tell it was in the thousands.

"Look, there's one of our banners" Tommy pointed it out to Nile. He thought it looked quite professional and stood out from many of the others.

The march's original route was to head directly passed the bookshop in Welling but after the back-and-forth negotiations, the head of the metropolitan police decided at the last minute to block this idea for safety reasons. The route would now take the main road that passed through East Wickham.

The march started peacefully but as the demonstrators approached the bottom of the hill in East Wickham where the bookshop was situated, the road was completely blocked by riot police. They had set up a wide exclusion zone with a large commission of riot and mounted police. They tried to divert the march to continue onto the newly planned route away from the bookshop.

Tommy felt his hand being tugged by Nile, he couldn't see through the thick crowd but he could hear the commotion. He was pulled closer to the edge and saw the police pushing the crowd back with their riot shields. This was not about crowd control. The police were becoming hostile as they openly incited the demonstrators by trying to provoke them to react. Tommy realised once he was at the edge of the crowd why Nile was intent on forcing her way through, Callan was in her sights. He didn't understand why she was so obsessed with him. Did she want to be with him, was he the distraction from him, maybe they had a thing in the past and she was still into him. He wanted to ask her, and if need be, demand an answer, but this was certainly not the time. He could visualise them arguing once this march was over and he would head straight for the first train back to Dundee, but for now, he would see out the day, watch the violence unfold and take away some good memories. His thoughts were soon interrupted when he nearly lost his footing after being pushed back from the pavement by the overzealous police. When he regained his footing, Nile let go of his hand and reached forward to grab one of the officers in an attempt to pull him into the crowd. She was forced back and smacked in the head by a riot shield which knocked her to the ground. Tommy grabbed her hand to help her to her feet and Callan appeared by her side to grab her other hand.

"Nile, what did I say? Cool it. They want us to react. You're playing into their hands."

Moments later all three of them were forcibly pushed back into the crowd by a team of officers with riot shields. Tommy looked around and he felt scared, the crowd had taken the bait and were now surging themselves back towards the police, including Nile, who was like a rabid dog, kicking their riot shields and screaming frantically at them. Tommy tried to pull her back but she was angrily pulling at an officer's riot shield, the officer, frustrated at Nile, lowered his shield enough to swing a punch to Niles's face.

"You fucking piece of shit" Nile screamed as the blood poured from her nose.

Tommy and Callan pulled her back into the crowd.

"Callan we need to do something, this is getting out of hand" Tommy gestured further up the line.

They both looked up to see the police stomping forward with their truncheons held high, ready to strike down on the demonstrators. Callan rushed closer to pull people out of the way to stop them from being hit, he was shouting at the police to back off.

"This is a peaceful protest, you lot are way out of line" He shouted.

His words went unheard as he was soon surrounded by the riot shields and beaten. Tommy managed to squeeze through the police and grab a hold of Callan and drag him back into the crowd.

"Thanks."

"You're bleeding."

Callan put his hand to his head and touched the blood "I'll be okay."

Tommy heard the sound of smashing glass and caught sight of more missiles being thrown overhead towards the police "This is madness."

Callan saw a gap in the crowd out of the way of the police "Let's go that way."

Tommy grabbed Niles's hand to lead her in the direction of Callan but she seemed reluctant to move.

"What are you doing, come on?"

"Why are you leaving? We need to stay and fight" Nile demanded.

Tommy was still holding Niles's hand and when he turned to face her, the police, on cue from a signal from their chief, made a coordinated surge forward towards the crowd. Callan, Nile and Tommy were soon crushed to the floor as the force and weight of bodies fell towards them. Tommy recovered and started helping others around him to their feet. The police surged forward again, only this time they had their truncheons held above their heads and began striking down on the bodies that lay helpless on the ground.

"This is absolute carnage. Let's step back, find the others and regroup" Callan insisted.

With Callan leading the way, the three of them moved slowly through the thick crowd until they were close to the tail end of the police cordon. Callan stopped and turned to face Tommy.

"Where's Nile?"

They both turned to see an officer dragging someone by the hair along the ground.

"Shit, that's Nile" Tommy shouted.

They both charged forward and pushed and pulled other officers out of the way to try to reach Nile. Tommy was only feet away when he was hit by a blow in the forehead by a truncheon. He fell to the ground and received a hard kick to the stomach that took the wind out of him. The officers made a circle around him and as he curled helplessly into the foetal position the officers laid into him with their truncheons. Callan was close by and knowing that Tommy had pulled him to safety moments earlier he knew he had to return the favour. He grabbed a hold of one officer and pulled him forward to make a gap and shoulder charged the next one to reach in for Tommy. As though in slow motion, the officer that Callan charged into, stumbled sideways into his colleague, who in turn, tripped over his foot and fell backwards. As he hit the ground the back of his head made a thud on the kerb. In the commotion, Callan managed to grab Tommy's hand.

"I've got you Tommy" Callan shouted as he attempted to pull Tommy free.

With the officer going down, reinforcements rushed from different directions and moments later, Callan and Tommy were handcuffed and dragged to a waiting meat wagon.

"The clashes with the police, or 'rioting' by the protestors as the press reported, went on for ninety minutes before the march was officially abandoned and the crowd dispersed. There were a few small skirmishes afterwards but they came to nothing. It was estimated up to 45,000 attended, seventy-four people were injured including twelve police officers. There were seven thousand officers present at the march with a cost of one million pounds. It was the same scenario as the Timex, they needed arrests to justify the cost of their presence but some had an ulterior motive."

"What do you mean?" Liam asked.

"Callan, they had been after Callan for a long time" Tommy confirmed.

Chapter 25

Tommy had been lying in the police cell for most of the day. There had been a lot of activity in the adjoining cells as they filled up with protestors but for the last few hours there had been silence. He was thinking that maybe he had been overlooked as no one had even bothered to check on him. He was constantly going over the events of the day and kept coming back to the image of Nile being dragged along the ground by the hair. He hoped she was okay.

It was late in the evening when the cell door opened and an older lady in a crisp clean police uniform with symbols on her lapels led him to an interview room. There was a tape recorder on the table and after pressing record, she introduced herself and asked Tommy to confirm his name and date of birth. Moments later, there was a slight knock on the door.

A young policeman stood in the doorway but did not enter the room "Mam, they're here now."

"Interview paused" The lady stopped the recording. "Excuse me, Mr Ross. A detective will be along shortly to continue the interview."

As she rose to leave the room Tommy asked "Can you tell me what I am charged with?" She glanced at Tommy but did not answer and let the door close behind her.

Tommy waited another fifteen minutes before two males in suits entered the room.

"Sorry for the wait Mr Ross, we've been waiting on other statements coming through before we could proceed. I'm Detective Baillie and this is my colleague Detective Clarkson" The taller of the two men said.

Detective Clarkson was slightly shorter than his partner but much stockier, both appeared a little rough around the edges.

They sat down in front of Tommy and placed a folder in front of them. There was no heading on the folder and it was left unopened.

“Can you tell me what I am charged with?”

“Well get to that shortly Mr Ross, first we need to ask you a few questions, would that be okay?”

“Sure.”

The record button was pressed again.

“This is Detective Clarkson and my colleague Detective Baillie continuing the interview with Thomas Ross about the murder of P.C. Shaun White.”

“Wait, what do you mean murder? I don’t know anything about any murder. I think you have me mixed up with someone else” Tommy immediately thought about the length of time he was in the cell and that they had mixed up the names at some point.

“Detective Clarkson put his hand up in a gesture for Tommy to be patient while Detective Baillie slid out an envelope from the folder. It contained several photographs and he placed one of them in front of Tommy.

“Can you identify the person in the photograph?”

“For recording purposes, Mr Ross has identified Mr Stanley Reid from a photograph presented to him by Detective Baillie.”

“Stanley, no his name is Callan and I hardly know him.”

“But you’ve been living with him in a squat up by way of Westminster for the last week or so?”

“Yes, along with many others.”

“And when did Mr Reid contact you about coming to live in the squat?”

“He didn’t, it was my girlfriend Nile who invited me to come down for a break as I was having issues back home.”

“Issues” Detective Clarkson gave him a concerned look “What kind of issues?”

“Child access issues, wait, where is this going? What has this got to do with the protest and why am I being interviewed about a murder? I haven’t committed or even witnessed any murder”

“We are trying to get a bit of background on your relationship with Mr Reid and the plot to kill or seriously injure a police officer.”

“Listen, I don’t and did not have a relationship with a Mr Reid. I came to London to spend time with my girlfriend?”

“Nile”

“Yes, Nile”

“You mean Officer Morrell.”

“What?”

“The female you are referring to as your girlfriend Nile is Officer Morrell.”

“Is this some sort of a wind-up?” Tommy smiled nervously but the two detectives were stone-faced as they keep their stare on him “Well whoever you’re saying she is, go and ask her, she’ll confirm why I’m here and that I was not involved in any murder.”

“Oh, we’ll ask her. But we have a few more questions first.”

Tommy sighed.

“Did you see Mr Reid strike Officer Shawn White?”

“I never saw Mr Reid strike anyone and I don’t know who Officer Shawn White is.”

Detective Baillie pulled out another photo from the envelope and placed it in front of Tommy.

“For recording purposes, Detective Baillie has shown Mr Ross a photo of Officer White.”

"No one struck him. He tripped over another officer's foot and banged his head on the kerb."

"So you are saying you do recognise Mr White?"

"I recognise him."

"And did you witness Mr Reid strike him intently causing his fatal head injury?"

"I didn't see Mr Reid strike him because he wasn't struck."

Detective Clarkson turned to Detective Baillie and let out a sigh "Okay I think we have enough for now. Interview paused" Detective Baillie pressed stop and they both exited the room.

It was over an hour later when the Detectives returned to the interview room "Look, I've asked you already. What am I being charged with?"

"Well get to that Mr Ross, but for the moment you have agreed to help us with our enquiries" Detective Baillie stated before he pressed the record button "This is Detective Baillie and my colleague Detective Clarkson continuing the interview with Mr Ross" He then nodded to Detective Clarkson.

"So Mr Ross, we have interviewed our colleague Officer Morrell, Nile, as you know her and we can confirm that she was working undercover to investigate a corrupt militant group led by a Mr Stanley Reid. She has informed us that she witnessed Mr Reid intentionally attack Officer Shawn White and that you Mr Thomas Ross were also a witness to this crime."

"No, no that is a lie."

"I know travelling from Dundee has been eventful and you were maybe taken in by Mr Reid's overpowering personality and also that your judgment of him may have been clouded…"

Detective Baillie interrupted "…You may have even been intimidated or even scared that what you saw today made you misinterpret what you originally told us…"

“…So we’ve made up a statement of what happened and we would like you to read it and see if it jogs your memory.”

Detective Baillie passed over a sheet of police-headed notepaper with a statement typed out. Tommy read it over and noticed a space at the bottom for him to sign.

“But that’s not what happened.”

“Thomas, there’s a dotted line underneath the statement. If you could sign it then we’ll have you out of here in no time.”

“I’m not signing that.”

“Thomas, now we know you have a soft spot for our Officer Morrell, she has already corroborated this statement, sign it and we’ll arrange for you two to meet up again and you can have your little bit of fun, there’s a good lad.”

“No, this is wrong, this is all wrong, none of that happened. Nobody wanted anybody dead and if that officer is dead, it was because he tripped over one of your colleagues.”

Detective Clarkson and Detective Baillie both faced each other before turning back to Tommy.

“Interview terminated” Detective Baillie stopped the recording and they both left the room.

Tommy was alone in the room for another thirty minutes before both detectives returned accompanied by an officer in uniform.

“Mr Thomas Ross, I am charging you with the murder of Mr Shawn White. You do not have to say anything, but it may harm your defence if you do mention when questioned something which you later rely on in court, anything you do say may be given in evidence”

“Wait, no, I didn’t murder anybody. The officer tripped.”

“Take Mr Ross back to the cells please” Detective Bailey instructed the officer.

"Nobody was murdered, he tripped" Tommy repeated as he was led away.

The cell door was slammed shut and Tommy burst into tears. He lay the whole night shaking and thinking over what had happened. The next morning his cell door was opened and a scruffy-looking man in a suit stood in the doorway.

"Hello Mr Ross, I'm Arthur Holloway, your appointed solicitor, I understand you've been charged with murder."

"I didn't murder anyone, he tripped and fell backwards and banged his head."

"Okay, we'll get to that, but first let's get you to an interview room so I can get a full statement from you and get up to date on things. The police will also want to interview you."

"They interviewed me last night, they've tried to get me to blame someone else and when I wouldn't sign their statement they charged me."

"So you've already given them a statement?"

"Yeah, I was in their interview room for hours last night. They said I was only helping them with their enquiries. Then they charged me."

"It's just that I have no record on file that they have even spoken to you."

"It was all on tape, they recorded it."

"I'll have to check that. Okay, come with me."

Tommy was escorted to a different interview room and went over his version of events for his solicitor. The whole time the solicitor was looking at his notes and comparing what Tommy was saying with the police report.

"They also told me my girlfriend Nile is a police officer, is that true?"

The solicitor flicked through a couple of pages on the report "As far as I am aware, Nile is Officer Yolanda Morrell. I take it you had no idea she was a police officer?"

"I didn't know until they told me yesterday. I thought they were lying to get me to sign their statement."

"Well according to this she is the main witness against you. Her statement says that she had suspicions about you when she was working undercover at the Timex strike and that you were planning a kidnapping and other various criminal activities."

"What does it say about the march?"

The solicitor scanned down the statement and turned the page "Oh here we are. She tried to pull you away but you were intent on hurting someone, Officer Shawn White was in your range and after you pursued him you used all your force to push him over."

"That's not what happened, why would she say that? I saw an officer drag her along the ground by the hair."

"This was put to Officer Morrell and her reply was 'Why would my colleagues attack me, dragging me by the hair, this is pure fantasy stuff'"

"Why would she say that? That is exactly what happened" Tommy was close to tears.

There was a knock on the door and Detective Baillie peered through a small gap "Are you ready?"

"I think my client needs a few more minutes."

Detective Baillie glanced at Tommy before closing the door.

"Just tell me when you are ready Tommy."

Tommy gave his eyes a wipe with his sleeve and took a few deep breaths.

"Now Tommy, you don't have to answer any of their questions. If you are unsure of what to answer just say 'no comment. Don't let them get you worked up. Are you ready to talk to them?"

Tommy nodded and the solicitor knocked on the door to inform the detectives that they were ready.

Detectives Clarkson and Baillie entered the interview room and introduce themselves. It was Deja vu for Tommy when Detective Baillie placed a new tape in the machine and pressed record.

"Where's the tape from yesterday?" Tommy demanded.

The two detectives gave each other a puzzled look.

"Tape, what tape?" Detective Clarkson asked.

Tommy looked to his solicitor who waved his hand in a calming motion "Continue with the interview please" He insisted.

After introducing themselves for the tape, Detective Baillie pulled out a folder and handed Tommy several photographs, each one is of Tommy on the Timex picket line in various poses pointing towards the strike-breakers.

"What the fuck is this?"

"We also have statements from a witness about a plot to kidnap a Mr Peter Hall."

"A witness, you mean Nile?"

"Are you referring to Officer Morrell?"

"You know exactly who I am referring to. This is a total fit-up. Yesterday you were trying to get me to sign a statement against Callan, and now because I refused, you are putting it all onto me" Tommy put his head in his hands "I can't believe this is happening. Look is there a way I can talk to Nile or Officer Morrell? I just need five minutes to talk to her and find out what is going on."

"I don't think that is possible at this moment in time."

"Please, I need to talk to her."

Detective Clarkson looked at Detective Baillie and nodded towards the tape.

"Interview paused" Detective Baillie stopped the tape and they both left the room.

"I don't think it's a good idea that you talk to her. She is the main witness against you."

"I have been charged with murder, I want to know why?"

The detectives didn't return and Tommy's solicitor left the room for an update on the situation. He returned half an hour later.

"What's going on? Am I going to get to talk to Nile?"

"She's unavailable."

"So what happens now?"

"The officers have informed me that they think you are covering for a Mr Stanley Reid. They believe he is the one that should be charged with murder so they have put a deal on the table. If you sign a statement that you witnessed Mr Stanley Reid assault Mr Shawn White, they will drop the charges, you will be free to go and return to court as a witness."

"No, no fucking way. That did not happen."

"You will be taken back to your cell for now and at some point you will go in front of a judge and you will be remanded."

"Remanded, until when?"

"You go to trial."

"What? I need to go on trial?"

"Well, that is a long way off, but yes, if you are pleading not guilty you will go on trial. They seem determined to pursue this as a murder charge which can be easily dropped to manslaughter."

“Manslaughter”

“If this happens they may push for voluntary manslaughter.”

“What the fuck is that?”

“It means they can’t prove you intended on murdering someone but you are capable of killing and due to the circumstances of the march, a provocation, or in the heat of the moment you intentionally killed Mr Shawn White and due to your background, it's likely they will prove intent.”

“So what do I do now?”

“You’ll be returned to your cell. So between now and tomorrow, you will need to think over your options, as once you go in front of the judge, it will be too late for the deal.”

Tommy’s solicitor gave a low knock on the door to be released from the room “I will be here first thing tomorrow. You can give me your decision then.”

“I can give you my decision now.”

His solicitor stood by the door.

“I did not intentionally or unintentionally kill or try to hurt any police officer.”

“Okay, well I guess we’ll see them in court.”

Chapter 26

"I'm guessing the way things turned out, it didn't go well for you in court" Liam commented.

"I was still of the belief that Nile would back me up, I was in denial that she was a copper until she turned up at court in her uniform. She was one of the aggressors towards the police that day, she wanted a reaction, it was a set-up for Callan but it was me that took the bait. From the moment I met her in the pub after the Timex demo she was playing me and I told her everything, all my early morning and late night antics, and then came the icing on the cake, the planned kidnapping, she stood in the dock and told the jury every single detail."

"But that had nothing to do with the officer dying."

"No, but they lost a colleague in the line of duty, so they needed someone to blame. I was made a scapegoat as other officers on duty that day filed up one after the other to testify that they saw me with rage in my face as I went for Officer White who was 'peacefully' trying to calm me down. They made me out to be some sort of maniac that went out that day with the intent to kill someone. I didn't have a weapon of any kind but I went out to kill someone."

"What about Callan or whatever his name was?"

"I hoped they would trace him and he would back me up but he couldn't be found. He was registered homeless. He wasn't on my or their witness list. My solicitor tried to hold back the trial for as long as possible until they found him but with me on remand the trial had to go ahead or they would have had to release me. I found out years later that Callan was working for someone high up the chain in politics. He was paid to organise that militant group and protest at certain locations, causing a bit of trouble to drive down the price of property or businesses so that a certain person can swoop in and buy it at a cheap price. He was a plant, each location they protested was hand-picked, of course, there were a few others thrown in to make his righteous cause seem worthy, that's why Nile was arguing with him about the BNP march, he was holding back, he didn't want to be there, it wasn't on his list or part of his employer's agenda. Anyway, the police knew what he was about but couldn't prove it. They wanted him charged with something, anything that would make him face a lengthy sentence to pressure him so that he would reveal his employer."

"What about the rest of them?"

"They would all go back to being filthy homeless squatters instead of being militants for hire."

"So if you knew who he was, why didn't he testify? Why was he not brought in for your appeal?"

"I found out he had a family, he was scared as they had been threatened. He realised that if they can go to the lengths of trying to pin a murder charge on him, what would they do if he stood up in court and called them out for lying? And would the jury believe him, I mean, just like me, he would have to be believed over the twenty-odd police officers that testified against me. Callan had strict instructions from his employer to disappear."

"How do you know this?"

"Once I had a 'position' in prison I asked a favour. I had to do a few bad things to get that information but for peace of mind, I needed to know. His one saving grace was that he refused to give a statement against me, which I know was put to him at the time."

"They didn't need his testimony, with the amount of police they had as witnesses, it was enough to go to trial. In court I was marked out from the Timex strike, they were allowed to produce certain photos of me on the picket line, but there were no photos of me standing with your gran, smiling and drinking tea or chatting with the other strikers, no, every single shot of me was in an angry pose, gesturing abuse towards the scabs. Their evidence in court, along with the psychology reports, was presented in a way to make me out as some sort of extremist. Then came their star witness, Martin"

“What did he have to do with it?”

“Nothing, but his evidence pushed the jury to think that I was some sort of psychopath. He painted a pretty rough picture of me.”

“I’m guessing that what happened to him was his karma.”

Tommy smiled “Yeah karma, that’s what it was. Turns out I didn’t even have to leave my cell to get my revenge on that slimy cunt.”

“I have a question.”

“Sure, what is it?”

“If you could go back to the time when you were offered a deal to give a statement against Callan, would you have taken it, knowing you would not have gone to prison?”

“Think about it Liam, if I had said, yeah okay I’ll sign it, they would have fitted me up alongside him, or I would have been threatened in some way just like Callan to stop me from telling the truth. Anyway, I couldn’t live with myself knowing I had helped put an innocent man in prison. Everything at that trial was a complete sham. Most of the evidence should have been thrown out. They were allowed to paint an unfair picture of me to the jury."

“What about Nile?”

Tommy turned away from Liam and stared into space as though in deep thought.

“I always thought Callan was playing a part, and of course he was, but so was Nile. The witnesses, the police, they all lied. The judge, before sentencing, labelled me an angry dangerous young man and gave me twenty years, I mean, I should have been out in ten for good behaviour but due to events inside, my parole was not only revoked, I had my sentence extended by two years."

Chapter 27

Liam arrived early to pick up Tommy. He was going over in his head how to tell his father what he had found out.

"Am I late again?" Tommy asked when he entered the van.

"No, not at all" Liam gave a sympathetic expression.

"What's wrong?"

"I found the crowd that's been terrorising the guy you chat to in the morning."

"Did you ask them to back off?"

Liam shook his head and pulled out his phone. He slid his finger along the screen until a certain page appeared "Is this the guy?" He held the phone in front of Tommy.

"Yeah that's the same guy" Tommy nodded.

"Take the phone and scan your finger up to read the article."

Tommy took the phone and gently scrolled up the screen to see the headline. He was in shock as he continued to read the newspaper article about his new 'friend.' He had been found guilty of touching up little boys when he was a football coach several years ago. He became close to the boy's parents and recommended some extra training sessions at another facility with an incentive of meeting some premier football players that the coach said he knew. This was all a ploy to be alone with the boy. Tommy scrolled faster to see paragraph after paragraph of details, but he had the jist of it and handed back the phone to Liam.

"I'm sorry Dad."

"What, you've nothing to be sorry for."

"I know. I'm sorry you had to find out like this."

"Don't be daft. Thanks for doing that for me. It's appreciated."

Tommy wasn't embarrassed easily, but he felt the Paedophile had shamed him in front of his son due to his deceived friendship. The embarrassment quickly turned to anger, and Tommy could easily hide his anger. He had previously been deceived in prison by these people, and now in his short time outside, he had been deceived again. In prison, they were dealt with in a ritualist way, but he was not in prison anymore and although his head was filled with hurting the Paedophile, was he worth ending up back inside?

It was still early, even for Tommy, his anxiety and haunting thoughts about befriending a paedophile had woken him after only a few hours of sleep. Usually, he would either lie awake or creep about the flat quietly so as not to wake Liam. Now that he was in his own place, he could get up, put the kettle on and have a cup of tea without disturbing anyone. He tried to switch off from his thoughts but it was no good. He finished his tea, got dressed and made his way out the door.

The streets were deathly quiet, there were no buses or delivery trucks at this time, and even the early risers were probably still contemplating getting out of bed. This was not Tommy's usual morning stroll, he was pacing, and it was as though his feet knew where to go without receiving the signal from his brain. He had covered the same route the last few mornings and each time he had talked himself out of it, that maybe he hadn't gone over the details enough or the information was wrong. He could always talk to him and tell him that he knows what he did and to never talk to him again, or he could even take a different route in the morning to avoid him, but he liked that route, he had it timed to perfection to see the sunrise on a good day. Why should he have to change his lifestyle because some filthy scumbag touched up kids? No, he had to go. Tommy weighed up his need versus want scenario and concluded that it was a need, and the need had to go.

He set off on his usual route but cut along the opposite side of the road when he approached the park. He followed the road around that took him straight to the block where the paedophile lived. There was no denying it was the correct block as it had 'Paedo' spray painted on the wall outside. There was a security entry door but even from a distance Tommy could see it had been forced open at one point and now vandalised beyond repair. Tommy walked by the block to a nearby side street, a particular house that was surrounded by a fence and a tall hedge, specifically chosen to stash a weapon the previous week. Tommy leaned over the fence and reached for the handle of the spade. His only thought was that if the spade had been removed, he would have taken that as a sign to walk on and forget the whole thing. With the fingers of his gloves he felt along the inside of the fence, when they reached the spade, Tommy gripped the handle and pulled it out above the fence.

After years in prison, Tommy had come to realise that anything could be used as a weapon. He had clocked the spade lying in another garden many weeks before and after eyeing it for the last few mornings, Tommy put his claim to it. He entered the Paedophile's block clutching the spade. The ground floor doors were untouched so Tommy walked up to the next landing. One door was covered in paint and what looked like footprints from a previous attempt at kicking the door in. For someone charged with the rape of a minor to the level that this man had been, there was a chance that his door would be reinforced so that even a battering ram would struggle to get through it, unless it split the door in half, but that would take a massive force. No, Tommy had no intention of forcing his way in, like in prison, he would lie in wait, and in this case, he stood in the darkened corner with his hood up.

The lights on the landing had been smashed a long time ago which saved Tommy another job. He waited over an hour until he heard one of the many locks on the door being turned. Three locks later, and with the release of a security bar that ran along the inside of the door, it gently eased open. Tommy stood still, he could hear the chain that connected the door to the side frame tighten. The Paedophile reached out slightly with a torch and Tommy did not breathe or move a muscle. He waited as the Paedophile finished his safety routine and unhooked the chain from the door. As he stepped out onto the landing clutching his dogs lead, a low "Psst" was heard behind him. The Paedophile turned slightly and was hit with a hard clunk to his forehead from the flat of the spade. He fell back into the hallway and made a thud on the floor. He was possibly already knocked out but Tommy quickly stepped over him and smacked him once more to the side of the head. He pulled the dog back in and closed the door. He knew the Paedophile lived alone but decided to give the flat a once over to make sure. There were piles of rubbish everywhere, and each room was more disgusting than the next. Other than exiting the flat and disposing of his outer clothing, he had no plan from here on in. He stepped over the Paedophile with the edge of the spade at his throat. With one hard strike, he could have easily decapitated him, and from what Tommy now knew about him, he deserved it, but Tommy decided he didn't need the anxiety of a murder hunt. Instead, he delivered several more blows with the flat of the spade before stepping back out on to the landing. He looked back into the hallway to see the blood splatters on the dirty walls. He left the spade behind and headed to the ground floor with the Paedophile's dog close beside him. Once he opened the main door to the block of flats, the dog bolted passed to the nearest lamppost. Tommy continued on the rest of his morning route, and would dispose of his gloves and outer clothing along the way.

As Tommy waited patiently on Liam to pick him up, his head was filled with the events of his last few days. There had been an appeal out for witnesses for the serious assault on the Paedophile but there was no description of anyone in particular. His thoughts drifted back to before his trial when the psychologists tried to get him to answer their questions, maybe they were right to try and analyse him. The only difference was, back then, he was innocent, but they were constant in their pursuit to categorise him as a psychopath or sociopath. He was neither, and even though he did have traits of both, this depended on the situation and most of these traits only surfaced once he had been imprisoned. Now, after recent events, he was questioning if they were right, was he a sociopath, or worse, a psychopath?

In the build-up to his trial, he was visited many times by a psychiatrist and he surmised that if he admitted or even discussed any of the traits suggested by the psychiatrist in any sort of detail they could easily make them fit his personality. He remembered the list, he had studied it, and top of the psychopath list of traits was 'likely to commit serious crimes' Of course he was, but that was due to his prison environment, now this had spilt into his life outside of prison, would he be committing these crimes if he had not gone to prison? No. Did he have a lack of remorse? Again this depended on the victim. Did he have a lack of deep emotional attachments? He did now, but not then. Narcissism, superficial charm, mimic feelings, Tommy was the complete opposite, dishonest, reckless risk-taking, presents normal to society. None of them fitted Tommy. The one that did stand out was organised in his criminal activity, he knew what he was doing was wrong but doesn't anyone that commits a crime? Do they care? They care more about getting caught. He was surrounded by psychopaths, and they weren't all classed as criminals. He remembered the list of sociopath traits, more likely to blend into society, repeat offender, pervasive lying and deception, physical aggressiveness, and lack of remorse, all traits Tommy had come across in his trial, from the people that stood in the dock in front of him, that lied under oath and used their position to put an eighteen-year-old kid in prison.

Liam sounded the horn on his work van and Tommy made his way down. He would usually ask what work was on for the day but he stared out the window at the heavy traffic.

"Is everything okay Dad?"

"Yeah fine, I just have a lot on my mind. Is everything okay with you son?"

"Yeah all good"

"I've been thinking, could set up that meeting with Ginge?"

"Are you taking the job?"

Ginge knew Tommy's capabilities from their time inside and Tommy knew the kind of work that Ginge was going to offer him. He had weighed up his need versus want and decided that he needed Ginge to get what he wanted.

"I think so, I'll talk to him, see what's what"

“His brother Ritchie was stabbed and killed the other night so I think he may be a little occupied.”

"Oh was he. That's a shame" Tommy didn't hide his unsympathetic tone.

"Yeah, he wasn't very liked so it's no great loss. It was some junkie named Jamie that did it, the whole of Ginge's crew are all on the warpath to get him."

Tommy knew who Jamie was but he did not let on to Liam. He saw him the day before as he hovered across the street from the chemist. It was late in the day when Ritchie finally reared his ugly head for his daily dose of Methadone, and this was when his path crossed with Jamie. Tommy was there to confront Ritchie for attacking Liam, but with a witness now in tow, he decided to tail them and hope they went their separate ways. Unlucky for Tommy, they both entered a house about a mile from the chemist, so Tommy had to lay in wait. If prison had taught him one thing, it was patience, he had hung around the chemist for most of the day and several hours later he was still watching the house. It was out of character for Tommy to be out at night but having his own place now, he didn't have to worry about Liam keeping tabs on him. The more time that passed, the angrier Tommy became which went against everything he was about.

It was dark and the street was deserted when things eventually kicked off. An argument had commenced in the house and a whole posse of junkies spilled out into the garden and then to the middle of the road. Tommy stood in the shadow of a large garden hedge opposite and listened as they argued over who stole Jamie’s drugs. Ritchie and Jamie were head to head and it soon became physical as they attempted to throw punches in between their pathetic wrestle. Jamie was shorter than Ritchie and much lighter so it was inevitable that Ritchie was going to use his weight advantage to overpower him. As they both stumbled to the ground, Ritchie was on top and the other occupants of the house decided it was enough and pulled Ritchie away. As Jamie rose to his feet, Tommy clocked the shiny blade being pulled from his pocket. He made a go for Ritchie and was only inches away from plunging the blade into him when one of the other junkies managed to pull him back. The others saw what was happening, grabbed the blade out of his hand, and threw it across the street. After a few more insults between them, they eventually went their separate ways and Ritchie was now alone. Tommy waited on the door to the house closing before emerging from the shadow of the hedge. He put his gloves on and walked over to the side of the road and pocketed the blade before continuing in the direction of Ritchie.

When Tommy finally caught up with Ritchie he knew there was only going to be one outcome. His original plan was to confront Ritchie about why he assaulted his son, but he hadn't waited all day and night for chit-chat. He could have maybe had it out with him about why he thought it necessary to beat up Liam after he had handed over the cash, but as Ginge had decided his punishment was to wash his hands of him, that didn't sit well with Tommy and this was going to be more of a message to Ginge than a punishment to Ritchie.

Tommy thought that out of respect, Ginge could have at least given him a courtesy call to apologise for his brother assaulting his son. Then there was also the fact that he was already angry at Ginge for recruiting Liam as one of his dealers in the first place. Tommy was also puzzled as to why Ginge would even let his junkie brother know about Liam dealing for him. If Ritchie was ever arrested and questioned under the stress of needing a fix, he would have easily given up that information. Tommy had figured that although Ginge was some sort of local gangster, his setup was sloppy, and if Jamie's blade hadn't become available when it did, the situation would eventually cause major repercussions for Liam and Tommy.

When Ritchie heard the footsteps behind him, he knew it would be Jamie. There was no way he was going to let it go. He knew, that Jamie knew, that it was him that stole his drugs. Ritchie had clocked the tiny wrap of tinfoil falling from his pocket and put his foot on it. When others in the house were occupied he bent down and slipped it into his shoe. It could have been anybody in that house that took it, but every one of them would have been too scared of what Jamie would do to them if he found out. No, he knew it would be Ritchie. As the footsteps got closer, Ritchie slowed down, he waited until they were right behind him before turning fast and grabbing Jamie with both hands.

"Right, you little prick...wait, who the fuck are you?"

Both Ritchie and his assailant stared at each other. Ritchie's eyes were full of hate and anger until he felt something pierce through his jacket and without any force, the blade slid easily into his body. His eyes quickly turned to shock as he realised he had been stabbed. The grip on his assailant slowly released as he fell to his knees and watched the dark figure casually walk away without uttering a word. With the handle of the blade still sticking out, Ritchie managed to crawl to his brother's house where he called an ambulance, but died on arrival at the hospital.

While there was an ongoing manhunt for junkie Jamie, Tommy had been informed about his evil past, and if he was going to be blamed for killing Ritchie, that was fine by him. Tommy was again weighing up the psychopath and sociopath traits with his own personality. He was happy to be where he was right now, it was exactly where he had dreamt of being during his whole time in prison, with his son, but his inner turmoil had been eating away at him since his release, an inner turmoil, caused by his time in prison, the rapes, the murders, and even the events that led up to his incarceration. He was no psychopath or sociopath but after recent events, he knew what he had become. Certain people's life choices had made Tommy what he was, and even though it had been twenty-two years, there was no time limit on justice, and no matter how long it would take him, they would reap what they sow.

"So what are we doing here?" Liam asked as he drove into a space in front of the dog kennels.

"Just wait here, I won't be long" Tommy smiled, knowing Liam wanted a different answer.

Tommy could hear the whining from outside the building. He entered and asked the young girl at the reception about adopting a dog. She asked some formative questions and took Tommy through to the back room where the dogs were located. There were not as many dogs as he imagined and he spotted the one he was looking for straight away. Tommy crouched down closer to the cage and the dog lifted itself on all fours and wagged its tail. The dog recognised Tommy and lifted its paw. He was after some broken biscuits.

“Can I have this one?”

Tommy compared his new companion to the loyalty of a dog in prison, he couldn't have a real dog in prison, but the next best thing was a human, the only problem was that no matter how much he trained a human, it was never going to be as loyal as a real dog.

Liam saw Tommy emerge from the kennels with the small dog on a pink lead and burst into a loud laugh "Suits you."

"It was the only colour they had."

Chapter 28

Tommy had received two of the addresses several months previously. He had travelled down to do some surveillance on them out but had not acted. He wanted to, but his need versus want scenario came into play and he walked away. Their time would come.

There were originally four addresses requested by Tommy, with one being his former lawyer, but luckily for him, he had died of natural causes several years before Tommy's release. There were many others that Tommy could have added to the list from his time in court but it was now narrowed down to three, Detective Clarkson, Detective Bailey and Officer Morrell.

Clarkson and Bailey had both retired from the force in recent years, so after a few discreet enquiries, they would not have been hard to locate. Officer Morrell on the other hand had been proving a little difficult. With Tommy now doing contract work for Ginge, he was making full use of his contacts to get what he needed. Tommy was a silent enforcer, he was now doing the same kind of work that he had done in prison to stay alive, only now, he was being paid a lot of money for it.

When all resources had failed, or a score had to be settled, Ginge would send in Tommy to take care of things. There were other types of contracts, like taking care of informants, but Tommy's favourite contract was Paedos. They were considered fair game, and for as much as he enjoyed cutting them up, they were worth the most money as they were outside contracts, and for this type of work, Ginge was only a middleman who took a small percentage for passing on the work to Tommy.

In the course of their now working relationship, Ginge had mentioned to Tommy about his brother Ritchie being murdered and eyed him as though he knew Tommy had done it. He told Tommy that Jamie, the person accused of the murder, and whose knife it was that killed Ritchie, pleaded that he did not do it, even when being tortured, he stated that when he turned to go after Ritchie, once their fight was broken up, he saw a dark figure appear from nowhere and assumed it was one of Ginge's men protecting him, so left it alone. Tommy knew this was a hint by Ginge to let him know that he knew it was Tommy that had done it. Nothing more was said, but the day would come when it would be dealt with, for now though, it would be a case of keeping your friends close and your enemies closer, and Tommy would use Ginge like he had used Liam all these years,

As soon as the third address was confirmed, Tommy packed a small rucksack and caught the first train early the next morning. He was hopeful he would be returning that same night, if not, the following day, depending on the time schedules. He arrived at Glasgow Central Station from Dundee and boarded the connecting train to Carlisle then another to Manchester. Tommy had no phone but had used Liam's without his knowledge to look up the address. He had taken mental notes on the area and chosen a certain landmark close by so that when he directed a taxi to the area, it would not arouse suspicion if things did not go to plan.

The only difference from his dry run to Manchester would be that his train would be travelling from London, and not Dundee. His main issue was cameras, since his time in prison, there were cameras on nearly every major street and building, some had several, pointing at every angle. Being aware of this since his release, his baseball cap hardly left the top of his head and with the peak always pulled down to hide his face, he rarely lifted his head in a built-up area. As with his Misophonia, which made him obsessed with certain noises, he now had an obsession with CCTV and made a great effort to avoid them, which was a good contribution in his new line of work.

It was raining heavily when Tommy stepped off the train in Manchester. This suited him, as along with his baseball cap, he could now pull his hood up over his head to help hide his face even more from any cameras that he had gone unnoticed. It had been a year since his release but he still could not get used to the idea that almost everywhere he went, every shop he entered, even walking along certain streets, there was always someone watching.

There was a line of taxis queued up outside the main exit to the train station and several people were walking fast in front of him, he held back to work out the number of people and each cab so that he did not have to double back on himself for the next cab in line. The driver was of Asian descent with a broken English accent.

"Maine Road please" Tommy accentuated his English accent.

The address Tommy was given was in Moss Side but he couldn't announce his intended location and Maine Road was the only familiar name he knew. Even though he was not a big football fan he had heard about the Maine Road Stadium from prisoners inside. Manchester City Football Club had vacated the Stadium in 2003. If the stadium was still standing, it would have served a purpose for the taxi driver to think this was his intended visit. It was only a short journey so Tommy made a point of staring out of the window in silence taking in the scenery to avoid small talk. By the time they reached the destination the rain had slowed to a drizzle but Tommy kept his hood up. He glanced up slightly and caught sight of several buildings with CCTV, he quickly took in each street name to familiarise himself with the map he had memorised, and with his head bowed low, he walked on until he reached the less busy streets. He slid back his hood now that the rain had completely stopped and it was relieving to lift his head and stretch his neck. He carried on anxiously as he was now only a street away. The area was not what Tommy was expecting. It was a built-up area and extremely run down. Tommy had pictured some expensive detached houses, placed in rows with landscaped gardens and high-class vehicles in each driveway. What he saw was a full row of attached houses with boarded-up windows and rubbish piled high by the bins in the street. He could see one car up ahead that had been burnt out with police-aware tape around it.

'Surely they wouldn't build new homes next to this' he thought.

He turned the corner to the address he was given and it was much the same. Did he have the correct address? Had they got them mixed up? Maybe it was a job they wanted him to do while he was down this way.

Not every door had a number but Tommy clocked the odd one here and there and stopped short once he worked out the rest. He turned back up the street and hovered on the corner until he could decide on how to go about this. The area, the type of houses, the whole scenario had thrown him. It was nothing to what he had imagined and this was why he always did a reconnaissance before any job.

His original plan was to enter the house, possibly from the rear and get the information that he wanted. The street was quiet except for a couple of people further down that had stopped for a chat. He slid off his rucksack and took out his bottle of water. He had bought it at the train station during the change-over in Glasgow. The lid was awkward and flipped to the side as he tried to turn it. He saw the nozzle and squeezed it to take a drink. The bottle made a crackling sound as it popped back into its original shape, and this made Tommy think about the time he became angry at Liam for his bottle making the same sound each time he took a sip. He was right, it was designed for squeezing. It was beginning to annoy Tommy that he couldn't take a drink without hearing the crackling sound.

He leaned down to put the bottle back in his rucksack and as he glanced up he saw a woman in the distance. She was with a young boy around ten years old and was walking in his direction. He tilted his cap upwards about forty-five degrees. There was no mistaking her. He could see the rolled-up cigarette in her hand, and the way she was dressed, she would have still fitted into her undercover role. As she got closer, Tommy pulled his cap back down to cover his face. He crouched down to his rucksack and pretended to search for something but his eyes were completely focused on her. He had read the file. She was a recovering crack addict and it showed. She went from a promising undercover officer to a full-blown junkie. Back when Tommy knew her, the one thing she had going for her was her pretty face and although Tommy could still see the features, she was rough, worn even. The twinkle in her eye was long gone. Seeing her after all those years was like blowing out a candle. She'd had three kids and been married twice but lived alone. Tommy wondered if her partners had been junkies also or if she had fucked them over like she had fucked him over.

In the seconds that it took for her to pass him, he had decided it was time to leave. He only wanted answers, answers as to why she took the stand and lied about what she saw. Was she pressured into it?

Was she promised a promotion or a cash bonus? Or even entry to a Special Branch? He had hoped she would have gotten something good out of her lies. He had travelled all this way for answers, answers that he waited years to hear. Now, after seeing her, whatever her reasons were for contributing to Tommy's imprisonment, they didn't go too well for her, and as Tommy could see, and from the file he read, fortuity had well and truly done its job.

Tommy picked up his rucksack and walked a few streets before flagging down a taxi back to the train station. The third address was now struck from his list.

Having already done his surveillance on the last two addresses, he had now returned to complete the job. As both Clarkson and Bailey had now retired, it did not take long to work out their routine. They had been partners for over thirty-five years and had joint family holidays together where they would sit in the sun with their wives and kids and grandkids to play the doting grandfathers, while their victims were rotting away in a jail cell. Victims, plural, as Tommy had later found out. The two detectives had set up many unsuspecting people over the years to close cases in their favour and had gained a lot of enemies over the years. Tommy found it hard to believe that no one had acted on them before now.

His plan was not going ahead until later that night, but after arriving so early he wanted to check out both addresses to make sure there were no changes since his last visit. He stood at the entrance to the cul de sac where Clarkson lived. The houses were large with open-plan lawns and long winding driveways.

During his previous trip, he had gathered a small pile of takeaway leaflets to get in close to check out the area, it had been a spur-of-the-moment idea but worked perfectly. Each door in the cul de sac had a camera and from under his baseball cap, he managed to spot several more discreetly placed to the side of two houses at either end of the close. When he reached Clarkson's house he saw him in his side garden playing with his grandson, being retired, Tommy always imagined him as a frail old man, but he still looked fit for his age, well-built and powerful. Tommy noted that he could be a handful if things did not go to plan.

Tommy thought of him telling his grandson bedtime stories of his time as a detective, especially one where he fitted up an eighteen-year-old boy and pressured other officers to lie in court so that the boy received a twenty-year sentence for murder, no, that was probably not a story liked to tell.

Tommy turned away from the cul de sac and walked the short distance to Bailey's house. It was a similar type of house, similar to Tommy, in that it was big and expensive, only this was situated on a main road and had a double garage but no front garden. It did however have cameras on either side covering each angle. Tommy walked to an adjoining street and followed the road around in the hope that it would take him to the rear of the house, but running parallel to Bailey's back garden was another row of large houses, all fitted with the latest CCTV.

'These were some paranoid times he was living in' Tommy thought. Paranoid or a possible guilty conscience that something or someone was going to catch up with them.

Tommy did not need to worry as he knew their routine. They religiously ventured out twice a week to their local watering hole and tonight, was one of those nights. They would consume considerable amounts of alcohol with their ex-police buddies and recount their time of distinction before returning to their lovely, expensive, secure homes only half a mile from each other.

The stone building was over a hundred years old, and from the outside, it looked dirty and dingy due to the weather, the inside had been upgraded over the years but it was still worn and dated. The upgrades had been implemented many years ago by the council for the owner to keep the building in line with the disability policy. A new toilet was fitted downstairs with wheelchair access and wider door frames. It had been classed as a working men's club which was a cover for Mason's lodge, but everyone knew it was a coppers drinking den.

Tommy hovered further up the street with a clear view of the comings and goings through the large wooden doors. He knew the ex-detectives were in there downing cheap pints of heavy, with whisky chasers and would stagger out of there at closing time. Tommy was counting the minutes. He had been calm and patient until he saw many of the punters leaving and there was no sign of Clarkson or Bailey. He was becoming anxious that they could be having a lock-in, as that would be a long night for Tommy and could put his plan in jeopardy. He had not ruled out them becoming too drunk to walk home and the barman putting them in a taxi.

Tommy's anxiety rested when he saw them appear in the doorway. There were three figures but the stranger was shaking their hands and patting them as though saying goodbye. Still observing from afar, Tommy watched the stranger walk in the opposite direction while Clarkson and Bailey talked loudly and laughed as they continued on their way. Two men, out drinking and enjoying their retirement, harmless and minding their own business, and while Tommy followed on slowly behind them, he saw them for what they were.

Tommy knew the route they would take to go home and also the exact spot where they would split to go their separate ways. He had worked out both distances and decided he had to go for Bailey first. He crossed the road and walked fast to get in front of him to reach the steel bar that he had strategically placed earlier and crossed the road once again. He was now walking towards Bailey with the steel bar by his side. When he was only feet away he slid the bar backwards and swung it sideways. In his intoxicated state, he did not see the steel bar before it smashed into his forehead knocking him to the ground. He was out cold. Tommy dragged his feet towards the kerb until the back of his knees were on the edge. He lifted the steel bar and smashed it into his kneecaps. Bailey did not make a sound, he was out cold. Tommy smashed the bar several more times. The blow to the head had saved him from the pain of the hits to the kneecaps, but it would not save him the anguish in the morning, when he would wake up in the hospital to receive the news that he would be in a wheelchair for the rest of his life.

Still carrying the steel bar, Tommy ran as fast as he could to catch up with Clarkson. He saw him in the distance and if he did not catch him before he entered his cul de sac, he might never get the same chance again, as once he turned that corner, he was all too aware that big brother would be recording everything from every angle. Tommy was breathing hard, and as he got closer he pulled out a plastic shank from his pocket and reached forward to plunge it into the side of

Clarkson. Tommy could have used any blade to do the job but this was a message. A message to Clarkson that being stabbed by a shank was a constant threat for the whole twenty-two years that he was inside and any inquiry about the assault would register that a shank is commonly used by prisoners.

Tommy's intention was not to kill but to wound him enough to slow him down. Once the shank was far enough in, Tommy snapped the handle so that the plastic could not be pulled out. It was strategically placed away from any organs so Tommy knew he would survive.

"What the fuck?" Clarkson turned to face Tommy.

As Tommy had suspected, Clarkson at first thought it was a punch and started swinging. Tommy stepped out of his way and waited. The shank would slow him down in a matter of seconds.

"You piece of shii..."

He swung a few more times and his breathing became heavier. He put his hand back to pull out the shank and soon fell to his knees.

Tommy savoured the moment. His pupils widened as he brought up the steel bar to head height, and with an angry force, he swung it hard into the side of Clarkson's jaw. Still conscious, he crumbled onto his side on the ground. Tommy stepped over him and watched as he mumbled to himself. He swung the steel bar high as though he was teeing off at a game of golf and let the end of the bar land flush to the front of Clarkson's face. It made a crunching sound that was a mixture of teeth and bone. Tommy lifted the steel bar one last time, and in a calculated move, he let it loose with more force than the first two. The sound was more of a thud than a crunch. He threw the bar to the side of the road. There was no point in hiding it or trying to place it somewhere. He would strip off his outer clothes and dispose of them where they would be destroyed.

Tommy casually walked off knowing that one would never walk again and the other would not talk. He had no guilt, no emotion, it was a job like any other, yes it was personal, but those two men not only took twenty-two years of Tommy's life, it was their own life decisions, and the chain of events that followed, that made Tommy what he had become, and they were now reaping what they sowed.

Printed in Great Britain
by Amazon

25255048R00126